Chef Charming

Chef Charming

Lyn Ellerbe

Chef Charming

Lyn Ellerbe

Copyright © 2021 Lyn Ellerbe Books

ISBN 978-0-9892464-7-7

Lyn Ellerbe Books

Facebook: Lyn Ellerbe Books
www.lynellerbe.com

*To Terry and Randy, for the gourmet cooking class fun
And to my wonderful husband who inspires me with his
humor, patience, and love.*

Thanks to my lovely daughters for being the first to read the story and urge me to share it. Writing this book brought back great memories of the gourmet cooking class that my roommate Terry, and our good friend Randy, took on a whim. To my friend Kathy and her daughter, thank you for your overwhelming encouragement.

It is my prayer that this story encourages Christian men and women as they work out their faith, stay true to their values, and enjoy the love that God so often shows us through our relationships.

1
Sleeping Beauty
and Chef Charming

A delectable aroma met the students as they opened the doors to the culinary arts building. Rori stopped to call her roommate.

"It smells delicious in here!" Rori teased her friend. "You'd better hurry. I'm pretty sure it's bacon!"

"I'm almost there." Even over the phone, Rori could tell Jessica was breaking into a run. The roommates had been looking forward to this beginner's gourmet cooking class for weeks. Both young ladies were set to graduate a week from Sunday, and had signed up for this community education class on a whim. Jessica was graduating with a degree in Culinary Arts so she was a little nervous about how Chef Marcus MacRae would react to one of the top students in the culinary program showing up for a novice class.

Rori had spent the last two years envious of Jess's prowess in the kitchen. If she could learn even a little bit of the magic, she would be thrilled. Even though this was a community class, the university allowed its students to take the class as an elective credit. They could take it for a letter grade, or just as an audited class.

Of course, this was not the best timing for Rori, but she was hoping the class would be a distraction to the pressure of her Graduate Art Show next Friday night. She spent most of her time in this building since the art studio was just downstairs. When she wasn't frantically finishing her paintings, she could usually be found on the third floor where she taught art in the afterschool program that the college offered for the children of faculty and staff.

Leaning against the wall of the food lab, relishing the aromas, Rori caught her breath. She had been in the studio and had barely had time to change clothes. Her painting overalls would not have made a good first impression. Maybe Chef would give them real chef's jackets; she laughed trying to picture herself looking so professional. She quickly wound her long curly hair into a somewhat organized bun and clipped it with a bright lime green barrette. Anyone that knew her very well would agree that the color suited her quirky cheerful personality. Plus, it perfectly matched the patchwork peasant skirt and green trimmed baby blue tank top she had paired with it.

This unassuming free-spirited artist had no idea how attractive she was. In her view, Rori was too tall and complained that her long dark blonde hair had a mind of its own. Although her curves were seemingly incongruent with her lankiness, they kept her from being termed too skinny. She always wondered too why God had given her a strange light blue set of eyes that would have been more striking set in a dark haired, olive-skinned complexion instead of the honey-touched one she was blessed with. Although Jessica envied what she called an adorable sprinkling of freckles across her nose, Rori knew she could never compete with her classically beautiful brunette, petite best friend. They secretly called themselves Mutt and Jeff.

"Hurry, hurry," Rori gestured frantically to Jessica who came sliding around the corner in her haste. Class had just started. The pair stopped at the doorway to try to control their giggling making their way, hopefully unobserved, into the classroom.

While they caught their breath, Rori glanced through the top glass-paned section of the door. The tall, auburn-haired chef was making his way around the room, introducing himself to each pair of would-be culinary masters. She heard deep, rich laughter.

When they had signed up for the class, she had asked Jessica what Chef Marcus MacRae was like.

"I only had him as a substitute for a couple of classes," her roommate explained that the chef had just joined the staff officially a couple weeks after Spring Break. "He seems nice, and has a bit of a dry sense of humor from what I remember. I think he knew Chef Jake in college," Jessica continued. Rori knew Jake Hampton, his wife Carla, and their daughter Zoe, from church.

"What does he look like?" Rori had pressed for more information. "Stunningly good looking like one of those network chefs, or more like Chef Boy Ar Dee?"

"Quite good-looking," Jessica had said, laughing at Rori's outlandish question. "If you like the Scottish Lord of the Castle kind of look."

Remembering that conversation now, Rori agreed with the description, at least from the back. Chef had continued around the room and moved to a place where she could now see his face. As he shook the hand of a young lady, a smile broke across his face. Rori caught her breath.

The dark reddish-brown hair was longer than the current close-cropped trends, and the neat, trim goatee gave Chef MacRae an air of royalty. "He looks like he could have been a real Scottish Laird, defending his clan from invaders," she whispered to Jessica. Jessica's description had been woefully inadequate. She had failed to mention that he was gorgeous. Thanks, Jess, Rori thought.

"Smitten are we, roomie?" Her roommate laughed, observing Rori's wide eyes.

"Let's get in there, I'm starving." Jessica tried to quietly open the door and sneak in. Unfortunately, the door was situated directly in Chef's line of sight as they stepped through.

"Nice of you to join us, ladies." Chef MacRae seemed startled as he glanced at the two young ladies. He nodded curtly. "Miss Johnston, I was surprised to see you signed up for the class, but welcome. And this is…?" He waited for Rori to introduce herself.

"Rori," she said, feeling her face turn red. "I mean, Aurora Sinclair. I'm Jessica, I mean Miss Johnston's, roommate." She couldn't believe how flustered she was. Normally she was cheerful and carefree, but this man intimidated her as no one else ever had. It was a surreal feeling.

Glancing to Jessica for support, she saw her friend was just as surprised at the chef's cold welcome as she was. They had observed his laughing and jovial manner as he made his way around the room, but now he had turned icy and brusque.

"Aurora? As in Sleeping Beauty?" Chef MacRae had now turned his full attention on her. She squirmed under his gaze. *I will never be late for another class in my life,* she thought to herself. *So much for first impressions.*

"Yes," Rori tried to regain her composure. Hating having to defend her unusual name, she was a tad irritated. "My mom is an elementary teacher and that particular story is her favorite." He ignored her, or so she thought, which caused her latent sarcasm to emerge. "Although I would never have taken you for a fairy tale connoisseur."

"Do you have a sister named Rapunzel, or Snow, or Cinderella?" Marcus seemed content to continue their conversation, despite her tardiness delaying the beginning of class. Unfortunately, he hadn't recognized her tone of irritation.

"Actually, no." Rori's rare temper flared. She smiled a falsely sweet smile at the disagreeable professor. "Her name is Gwen."

"As in...?" Marcus continued, unaware that their conversation had drawn the attention of the class.

"Guinevere," Rori answered. "My father is a Professor of History. Mom got to name me, so he got to name my sister."

Struggling to regain his composure, Chef Marcus reverted to curtness.

"Well, Princess Aurora," he said, and watched her blush at his sarcasm. "So glad you woke up in time to make it to class. I'd appreciate it if you would find time in your busy schedule, Your Highness, to make it on time tomorrow night."

"Yes, Chef," Rori ducked her head and nodded. She was stunned at his rudeness, not that it was unjustified. She and Jessica had disrupted class with their lateness. Rori was such a positive, upbeat person, to a fault some of her friends said, that encountering someone so much her opposite left her speechless. Her family and close friends would laugh at the idea of her speechlessness, even under extreme circumstances.

"I'm so sorry," Jess whispered as they made their way to their station. "Like I told you, I've only had Chef MacRae as a substitute in my pastry class. I thought he was really nice and funny then. Maybe he's just having a bad day."

"Or a bad life," muttered Aurora. She fought back uncharacteristic tears and silently prayed for intervention.

'Lord, help me endure this trial. I know it may seem trivial, but I think that I'm in the class for a reason since it was such a fluke for me to be able to sign up for it. Please show me what that reason is so I can put up with the verbal abuse I appear to be in for...and please help me be kind to this man who seems to have decided to dislike me so quickly.'

2
Is it Crapes or Crepps?

Apparently, the incident was not of enough importance to cause Marcus any hesitation as he began the instructions. "You will see on the screen behind me a list of safety issues," Chef MacRae immediately began, "Each of you has two copies of this at your station. On both copies, please initial beside each item and sign at the bottom. I will come around and collect one of the signed forms as I take attendance. The other form should be placed in your binder."

Rori pulled her binder from her superhero backpack, not realizing what an eccentric combination her hippie-like attire, bright neon hair clip, and her masked avenger backpack made. She tried to be as quiet as possible, hoping not to attract any more attention. Unfortunately, in her nervousness, she dropped her pencil case as she pulled out the notebook. Of course, since she was an artist, it was not an ordinary zippered, canvas pencil case. It was bright, shiny, and metallic. Perfect for making a lovely and loud clanging noise.

Chef turned towards her table at the clamor. "Problems, Princess?"

"No." Rori groaned and Jessica for some reason found the situation quite funny. Rori knew Jessica well enough to know that her sudden interest in the bowls lined up on their station meant Jess was trying to hold in her laughter.

"Good." Chef dismissed her with a look of impatience. Turning to the rest of the class, he gave further instructions, "You can also begin reading your recipe and instructions so we will be ready to begin as soon as possible."

"Yum," Rori whispered to Jessica who had finally composed herself. "It's crepes."

"Or crepps," Jess giggled pronouncing the word in her best over exaggerated French accent. The surreal tension of the first half hour of class caused Rori to be slightly giddy. She giggled at Jess's antics. Of course, the chef chose that very moment to step to their station so he could collect their paperwork.

"Something funny, ladies?" Chef MacRae asked.

Jessica jumped almost to attention, her military upbringing, and culinary experience coming into play. Aurora on the other hand had found her voice and her innate tenacity again.

"Yes," Rori replied as she met the chef's serious striking green eyes with her dancing ones. She was not going to let this man intimidate her. Plus, maybe he just needed to laugh more. "We were wondering, is it pronounced *crapes* or *crepps*?"

"Whichever you prefer," the chef clipped out. "Now if I may check your names off so you can get to work. I know not everyone takes cooking as seriously as I would like but please try to maintain some discipline in my kitchen. Miss Johnston, I expected more decorum from you."

Immediately regretting having gotten her best friend in trouble, Rori tried to make amends.

"I'm sorry, Chef," she interjected quickly. "That was all my doing. Please don't hold my immaturity against Jessica. She really does take cooking seriously and she is very good at it. She is graduating in the top two percent of the culinary arts program and has a promising future. She cooks for us all the time and even volunteers at the homeless shelter once a week, cooking them gourmet meals with the pantry items. She...."

"Enough," Marcus cut in. "You've made your point. Now please concentrate on getting your ingredients ready."

Jess had buried her head in her hands about halfway through Rori's ramble. Those that knew her roommate well found Rori's endless chatter endearing. Rori only got out of control when she was nervous. Obviously, that was the case tonight.

"Sorry," Rori mumbled, *I seem to being saying that a lot tonight, she thought to herself.* Marcus handed her the roster. While she signed her name, and added her email address and phone number, he told them he'd be communicating class issues solely by email, but requested their phone numbers, in case he needed to get class news out quickly.

"My email and phone number are on the class syllabus," he added as she slid the clipboard toward him.

"I hope he's in a better mood tomorrow, otherwise this class is going to be miserable," Jessica said. As they began to measure and prepare their ingredients, she added, "At least for you, Rori." She chuckled at her friend.

"Funny." Rori rolled her eyes. "We can only hope."

Chef Marcus returned to his teaching station and reclaimed the class's attention.

"You should be done with your preparation, which we call *mise en place*," he said.

Rori grinned excitedly at her partner. Jess always took time to explain the terms and skills they saw on their favorite food shows. Despite being quite a novice in the culinary realm, Rori was addicted to cooking shows. That was fine with her roommate, too. One of the main things Rori was looking forward to in this class was practicing all the skills she had watched so often. The few times Jessica had let her 'help' with a practice dish had ended in near disaster so she was hoping to improve. Not that it would take much, she thought. Her skills had nowhere to go but up.

Chef MacRae spent the next half hour discussing and demonstrating basic techniques, making sure the entire class had simple measurement and mixing skills. He had gathered the students around his central station in the middle of the food lab. The college had recently won a grant and had invested a significant amount of the money on the latest in high tech equipment.

Marcus chose random students to attempt each skill. Jessica demonstrated fine chopping skills, the most advanced of the introductory techniques. Of course, she did wonderfully and winked at Aurora as she returned to her side. Chef demonstrated mincing, julienne, coarse chopping, and dicing, and then asked volunteers to try. Rori was not about to raise her hand. At the end of this instructional time, chef sent the novice cooks back to their stations to practice their skills on the ingredients they would be using in their crepes.

"I will come around and check your progress," Marcus said. "I may also ask you to demonstrate one of the techniques to make sure you are progressing in your learning. We'll spend ten minutes on these skills and then I will demonstrate the actual crepe making." As he was speaking, he cleared up his station. He was meticulously clean about his work area and had made the point earlier in the class.

"He's such a neat freak. I hope he never comes to my studio," Aurora said to Jessica. "I'm not the messiest one down there, but just the general chaos of all the supplies would probably render him apoplectic." At the thought of annoying the handsome, distinguished chef, Rori added, "Hmm, then again, maybe I ought to invite him down!"

"Be nice," Jess laughed.

Chef MacRae made his way around the lab, stopping at each of the eight stations.

"Are you ladies ready?" He stood before them. "Miss Johnston, you are excused from this requirement, but

Miss," he hesitated as he checked the roll for Rori's last name, "Sinclair, show me a julienne chop of this carrot, please."

Aurora had never been so terrified in her life. The normally cheerful, vibrant young woman gulped. This class was a terrible idea, she thought to herself.

Her hands trembled noticeably as she attempted to duplicate the chef's perfect cuts. She did not do well at all and could see the frustration in his face.

"I'm sorry," she said.

"You seem to be saying that a lot this evening," Chef Marcus muttered.

"You make me nervous," Rori blushed, realizing she had accidently spoken her thoughts aloud.

Marcus hesitated noticeably. Her statement seemed to confuse and surprise him.

"Well, I guess you will have to learn to deal with my ominous presence, now won't you?" His tone was mildly sarcastic. "Watch me one more time."

He moved around the table to her side and demonstrated the cut once more, gesturing for her to try at the same time. Still not satisfied with her nervous attempts, he reached across her, placing his hands over hers.

"This is the correct way; calm, up and down consistent rhythm." He moved her hands as he spoke. "Now you try. He remained beside her, watching over her shoulder. "Better," he said, and then abruptly moved to the last two students.

Jess's eyes were round with surprise and Aurora stood in stunned silence.

"I've never been so scared in my life," Rori whispered. "Why, oh why, did I ever sign up for this class?" Her words didn't reveal what she was actually feeling. She wasn't ready to admit to herself, much less to her roommate, that his touch on her hands had sent a course of electricity through her. She had felt a strange feeling of loss when he moved away. This is silly, she thought. I cannot possibly be attracted to this man. He can barely tolerate me.

"I think he should change his name." Anger in her voice, Rori's good nature had finally been pushed to the limit.

"To what?" Jessica realized her roommate was finally showing some of the same righteous anger that she herself felt at his mistreatment of her roommate. "Sir Frowns a Lot?"

"That's a good one," Rori giggled, "but I think Chef Charming fits him better."

Jessica's laugh turned the head of fellow students and earned her a scowl from the chef, but she didn't mind. Chef Charming and Sleeping Beauty she thought, perfect match.

The rest of the class was a blur. Chef demonstrated the tricky mixing, pouring, and cooking of the crepes. All the stations had struggles and there were plenty of groans and laughter the rest of the evening. Even Chef seemed to lighten up a little bit. Jessica made Rori do the crepes.

Jess had worked in a French restaurant during her culinary arts internship, so it was a skill she had already perfected.

Each station had to get approval of the chef before plating and tasting their masterpieces. The class shared their recipes and tasted each other's creations. They had all chosen various combinations of the ingredients for the filling. Jessica's favorite was a chicken and broccoli Alfredo variation made by one of the pair of graduate students at the neighboring table. The young man was quite handsome, so Rori teased her.

"The crepe was probably inedible," she teased, "but the cook is scrumptious, right?" Neither coed realized Chef Marcus MacRae had overheard their banter. He was fully aware that they were talking about John Liu, the young man whose station adjoined theirs.

Marcus had seen the two girls flirt outrageously with the young man. Not that it mattered to me, he told himself. He was a professor and they are students, so their relationships are none of my business. If he were honest with himself, he would admit that he was very interested in the relationships of one of them. Chef Marcus spent the rest of the evening in bad humor.

"Tomorrow night we will be exploring the world of spices," Chef spoke over the noise of the clearing of their stations. The students stacked their dirty utensils and cutlery on the designated station. Each team was to take a turn washing and storing all the equipment away at the end of class.

"We'll be doing this through a series of rice dishes. Rice is an ingredient common to many, many cultures and it will give us a perfect palate for exploring. I need a volunteer to come in early to start several pots of rice so we have enough to begin class. Please see me afterwards if you are free to do so."

The chef stood at the door and handed out the vocabulary assignments as the students left. Rori hopped into the line to take advantage of this opportunity. She courageously planned to volunteer for the rice assignment. Her studio and the after-school program were all in this building, so it was no problem for her to come in half an hour early. With her major art show on Saturday night, she would welcome the excuse to get out of the studio. Plus, maybe this would win her back some points with Chef Charming.

"I can come in early to do the rice," Rori told him as she took the assignment papers. "I'm here in the building all day anyway, so it's not an inconvenience."

"Fine." Chef accepted her offer but seemed perturbed. "Be here at six o'clock."

Rori's conscience could not find rest. At one o'clock in the morning she rolled out of bed, turned on her computer and pulled out the information page from the cooking class. Do it before you lose your nerve, she told herself.

Dear Chef MacRae: I want to apologize for causing problems in class tonight. I will try to get my act together

and be better prepared tomorrow. Please forgive me.
~Aurora Sinclair

She hit send and crawled back into bed.

3
Spice and Rice

The next evening at precisely the required time, Rori burst through the door.

"I'm not late, am I?" She had been caught up in one of her final paintings and had lost track of the time. She didn't even have time to change out of her painting clothes.

Marcus looked up from his notes. The fairy woman standing before him caused his heart to miss a beat. Her long hair spilled over her shoulders. Tattered overalls splattered with paint covered a baby blue tank top. She even had paint on her elbow and cheek. He reacted in self-defense.

"Pushing punctuality to the line, aren't we?" Hearing his own voice, he knew it was harsh but he couldn't seem to help himself.

Marcus had unwillingly admitted to himself that for some bizarre reason he was drawn to this strange young woman. If he was going to survive these next twelve days, he had to make sure she did not suspect his attraction. He had complained about her last night to his friend, fellow professor, and confidant, Jake Hampton. Jake had reminded him that there was no restriction on relationships between adjunct professors and graduate students, but Marcus still did not want to go down that road. He was serious about his faith and knew that he could never have a relationship with someone who did not share his values. He had no idea what this magical being's belief system involved. He had even complained to Jake that he had doubts that she was even of this world.

"You have it bad, my friend," Jake had laughed. "I may have to come by your class tonight to see this creature."

Marcus laughed wryly to himself imagining what Jake would think of her if he saw her right now. She wasn't the delicate being he had described from last night. Still, he marveled that someone could make baggy paint-splattered overalls and disheveled hair look so enticing. He vowed to keep his distance tonight.

He pointed her to the pantry supplies and began pulling out the necessary cooking pots.

"You do know how to make simple white rice, correct?" Marcus asked her. He felt a pang of guilt as he saw her wince at his biting comment.

"Yes." She nodded, trying to guard herself from his jabs. "How much do you need and do you want me to put any seasoning in it?" She normally put salt in the water when she made simple rice dishes for herself.

"Put a half a teaspoon of salt per four cups of water in each pot. That is less than normally added, but we will be adding a lot of different spices to all of it."

He moved back to his papers, trying desperately to dismiss her presence. *Why did I ever agree to let her come in early?*

"Lord, help me here!" He sent up what his high school youth pastor had called a 'Flare Prayer.' Marcus knew that he should have spent more time spiritually preparing for this battle before class, but now he was desperate.

In answer to his anxious plea, Marcus heard Chef Jake Hampton's familiar whistle.

"Thank you, Lord," Marcus breathed, unaware that Jake was already standing behind him.

"No, it's just me," Jake quipped. "Although some of my students do think I have superpowers." Marcus ignored his friend's attempt at humor but appreciated the timely rescue.

"So, is that the fairy princess?" Jake nodded toward the station where Aurora was preparing the rice. "She's not dressed quite like I'd expect from Sleeping Beauty."

"Yes, but keep your voice down," Marcus said. He admired and loved his friend but his clowning around was not appreciated tonight.

The two had attended the same culinary institute and both had graduated four years ago. Chef Hampton had immediately been hired as an assistant professor when the culinary arts program at the college began the following fall. Marcus had taken a position as an executive chef at an upscale ski resort. The friends had stayed in touch, though, and when this adjunct professor position opened, Jake encouraged Marcus to apply. As the program at the college gained popularity, he knew that it was likely that the temporary position would turn into a permanent one. He was thrilled to have his friend here.

"She looks harmless to me," Jake said, but he could only see the back of her head as she was filling the pots with water before setting them to boil. "I wouldn't have thought the big bad wolf was afraid of Goldilocks."

"You're mixing up your fairy tales atrociously," Marcus pointed out.

"Rori!" Jake exclaimed as the young lady turned around. He crossed the room and greeted one of his favorite church friends with a big hug.

"You know her?" Marcus gaped at his friend who proceeded to help Rori move the large pots onto the burners. Jealousy not just for the relationship, but also for the display of casual affection, swept over Marcus.

"Rori and I are old friends from church," Jake explained to his flabbergasted friend. Rori nodded and smiled at her chef instructor. Maybe having a mutual friend will help him get out of his bad mood, she thought.

"Plus, she is Zoe's *favorite* teacher at preschool," Chef Jake continued. Rori rolled her eyes as he added, "Rarely does a day go by that Aunt War-ee isn't a topic of excited conversation at our house." The proud father purposely mispronouncing the young teacher's name just as his four-year-old daughter did.

"I love Zoe," Rori admitted to mutual affection and grinned. "She's a gem. Must take after Carla."

"Ha, ha, ha," Jake retorted, inwardly admitting his wife was the main reason they had such a delightful little girl. "So, I see you got roped into sous chef duties tonight. What did you do wrong to deserve having to spend more time with Chef Grumpy here?"

Rori was amazed at the natural teasing and obvious kinship between the two friends, although Chef Marcus did seem uncomfortable being the center of attention.

"Oh, no," she said, trying to fix the damage Jake was unknowingly doing. "I volunteered. I practically live in the building anyway, so it was logical for me to help out." She hoped she sounded calm and nonchalant. Her feelings were anything but indifferent but knew she could not let these two men know it.

"After I get these boiling, is there anything else I can do?" she asked. "Do you want me to stay and guard the pots, or can I go change clothes? I was trying to finish up a layer on one of my paintings and didn't want to be late so I didn't get to change."

"No, you have to stay." Chef MacRae's curt reply was instantaneous. "Sorry, it's part of the job." Jake raised his eyebrow, suspicious of his friend's motives. They would definitely talk later.

"That's okay," Rori agreed, pinning a syrupy sweet smile on. "I'm here to do your bidding." If he was going to make this hard, she was not going to help him out in any way. She would be so agreeable that any criticism of her would seem mean and petty.

Jake barely covered up a guffaw as he saw Marcus pale. This is going to be fun, Marcus's traitorous best friend thought.

Thankfully, Jessica picked that moment to arrive. She had purposely left work early so she could be there for Rori as she braved the lion's den, as Rori had termed the food lab. The auburn hair and ruddy complexion Marcus had inherited from his Scottish ancestors lent itself to the imagery. Jessica suspected that Rori Sinclair was slightly, if not more than slightly, infatuated with this tall handsome chef.

"Did I miss anything?" Jess whispered to Rori who was patiently watching the pots begin to bubble, ready with the uncooked rice.

"Nope." The one-word answer conveying volumes to Rori's friend.

"That bad, huh?" Jess put her backpack away and slipped on her chef's coat.

"Yup," came another one-word response.

Jess pulled Rori's chef coat from the hook at their station, urging her to put it on. Obviously, she had been too distracted when she got here to remember it. Jess was surprised that Chef had left the gaffe slip. Although her experience with him had shown his kinder, gentler side, after last night she thought that his mood in this class would be different.

"Thanks," Rori mumbled as Jess handed her the coat. The culinary department provided inexpensive coats for the students to rent, finding it lent them an air of professionalism. Of course, Jess had her own more expensive one. Rori teasingly called her a culinary snob.

"Wow," Jess was now beginning to be concerned. "Three one-word answers. He has you rattled, doesn't he? And don't just say, 'Yes,' or I'll bop you!"

Rori grinned as her natural optimism won out. "Ok, how about, 'yes, he does.' Is that better?"

The friends both glanced at the door as Chef Hampton finished giving his friendly advice. Trying to appear stern, but still finding the situation hilarious, Jake had to duck as he left the room, barely missing the hard sesame roll Marcus had playfully launched at him.

"Get out of here. I can handle this on my own." Rori heard the cryptic remark Marcus made to his friend.

"Sure," Jake called through the open door, picking up the pastry and tossing it back to Marcus. "Let me know how that works out, will you?"

As Marcus turned around, he saw Rori watching him. Hopefully she did not know that she was the topic of conversation.

Slightly embarrassed at having appeared to be eavesdropping, Rori blushed and tried to look busy, cleaning up an already spotless station. She wished she could keep her art area this neat. It never failed, though, as the best-laid plans dissolved into chaos when an inspiration hit her and she struggled to get it on canvas as fast as she could. Sometimes it was hours later before she realized she had created total pandemonium out of her orderly intentions.

As the rest of the class filed in, Chef MacRae called them to his station.

"Tonight, we are going to explore the different spice profiles common in cuisines from around the world," he explained. "Each pair of you will choose one of the spice profiles to highlight. The baskets on the side table have the necessary ingredients, recipes, and a description of the region's cuisine. Since Miss Sinclair so graciously came early to prepare our rice, she and Miss Johnston will be allowed to choose their cuisine first. Ladies."

"Let's get Moroccan," Jess suggested as they stood before the table. Rori had no opinion on the matter, still smarting over the inflection in Chef's voice when he said, graciously. She wondered if she had imagined it or if the rest of the class knew he had it out for her.

"Fine." Rori shrugged and helped gather their supplies.

Great, thought Jess. One word again. This was going to be a long night.

"Thank you, John and Calvin," Chef nodded to the two young men at the station next to Rori and Jess. They were the last pair to share their dish as the class time was approaching an end. Chef MacRae had asked each group to give feedback to their classmates. John and Calvin's Mexican rice dish was a big hit with the class so far. Rori and Jessica were the only partners who had not given a critique yet.

"We're next," Jess whispered. "I'll take it, if you want."

"Yes, please," Rori's heart was pounding at the thought of having to speak coherently under the ominous stare of Chef Marcus.

"And, you, Miss Sinclair?" Of course, Chef did not let her off the hook, turning to her with his intense green-eyed stare. "Do you have anything to add?"

"It was yummy?" Rori answered, eliciting laughs from the rest of the class.

"Perhaps you could enlighten us as to exactly what you considered 'Yummy' if it wouldn't be too much trouble," Chef insisted. This woman infuriated him and fascinated him at the same time. He was sure she knew he was not happy with her, yet she turned it into a joke. It was going to be a long two weeks.

Rori jumped as Jess pinched her and whispered, "Behave!"

"I liked how the dish was rich and hearty without being too spicy," Rori offered, her statement almost a question.

"Very good," Chef moved back to the center of the lab, almost dismissing her comment.

"Tomorrow we will be further exploring these regions through stews and other dishes," Chef said, preparing to dismiss class. "We'll be reviewing knife skills and you will also have your first quiz on the safety sheet and culinary terms. Please come prepared."

She had not seen his response to last night's email until after the second class.

Dear Miss Sinclair: Thank you for your apology, though it was unnecessary. I hope you enjoy the class. ~Marcus

Those few words in no way conveyed the battle that had raged within Marcus over his response. He literally had written and deleted over twenty attempts. His first was along the lines of: *I think I am losing my mind. When you walk in the room, I turn in to an unrecognizable monster. You are the bane of my existence but I can't imagine coming to class tomorrow and not having you there.* Thankfully, he had not sent that one, but opted instead for a safer, indifferent message.

She was checking her mail in the studio, having returned to finish cleaning up. Jessica was going to get coffee with John and Calvin, their neighbors in class. They promised to return so they could walk Rori back to the apartment.

Rori was surprised that he had even responded, but for some reason was disappointed at the stoicism conveyed in it. She wasn't arrogant, but also wasn't used to people disliking her. I guess I just rub him the wrong way, she thought. Still not willing to let him continue in his total dislike of her, she typed a quick response to his email:

Deaf Chef, I am enjoying the class and learning a lot. Thank you for letting me help with the rice tonight. I hope, too, that Chef Hampton doesn't tell you any ludicrous stories about me. He, Carla, and I had a crazy experience at one of our Bible study outings last fall. My part in the antics is quite embarrassing to recall but I'm sure Jake will make them sound worse than they really were. ~Aurora

The new mail notice beeped loudly. He must have been sitting at his computer, because his response was almost immediate.

Dear Miss Sinclair, I am glad you are not letting my bad moods affect your learning experience. I'll be sure to pick Jake's brain about your 'antics'. And outside of class, it's Marcus, not Chef. ~Just Marcus

4

Stewed and Steamed

Aurora was optimistic heading into class the next evening. Their secret emails gave her hope. She had not told anyone, not even Jess, about the two brief computer conversations. It was almost like they were treasures she wanted to keep for her own.

Before class, Jessica joined Rori in the studio.

"So, Chef Charming is Jake Hampton's best friend," Rori sighed. She was lazily painting a spare canvas, wasting time before class.

"Isn't that weird," Jess said. "I knew that they knew each other from college but didn't realize they were close. Marcus must be the college friend Jake talked about on the ski retreat. The one that he got into all sorts of trouble with."

Rori had quickly painted a colorful backdrop of swirls on a small canvas. The colors were muted, but the broad strokes indicated her restlessness. Glancing at the clock, she saw she had time to outline a castle in the distance, making it seem to rise from the clouds of colors.

"Wow, that looks nice," Jess jumped off her stool and looked closer. "It always amazes me how you can do that so quickly. It looks like a fairy tale castle. Like where Prince Charming or Princess Aurora would live."

"Great," Rori rolled her eyes. "I'll call it *Aurora's Castle*. If I even finish it. I really have a couple other pieces I absolutely must finish for the show. I don't even know why I started this one."

"Oh, I do," Jess teased. "You've got Prince Charming on your mind. Or is it *Chef Charming*?" She ducked as Rori threw a paint rag at her.

"That's not funny," Rori said.

"I think it's hilarious," Jess replied. "Seeing you thrown so off balance by the handsome chef is quite entertaining."

"Off balance is an understatement," Rori said under her breath.

"You are one of the most content people I know," Jess continued. "I wonder what it is about Marcus MacRae that makes you so nervous. Have you ever reacted to a guy like this before?"

Rori fell unusually silent. Obviously, Jessica's question had hit a tender spot, but Rori quickly gathered her emotions back into check and laughed.

"Oh, all the time," she said. "I fall in and out of love almost daily. I should be over Chef Marcus by tomorrow, when the next pretty face comes along."

"Yeah, right," Jess said. She was curious about Rori's reaction but knew now was not the time to press for the truth.

"Help me clean up so we aren't late to class," Rori said, laughing off her roommate's teasing.

Marcus saw Rori and Jessica enter about five minutes before class time. He was unsure how to behave. That he was attracted to her was obvious to him, but he needed to hide that from the rest of the world. Jake had tried to feed him a line about there not being restrictions on adjunct professors and graduate students, but it still did not feel kosher to Marcus. He was certain Aurora Sinclair would have been shocked had she been privy to the conversation Marcus had with Jake earlier that day.

"I know true, godly love is not based on physical attraction," Marcus had pointed out to his friend, "and that's why I'm struggling. When I saw her, it was like a movie special effect where everything else faded away.

Jake had barely managed to hide his laughter form Marcus.

"And that has worked out so well for you, now hasn't it, Mr. 'I've Got This Under Control'?"

Marcus was willing to accept the teasing because he knew Jake was trying to help. He just wanted answers, or relief from this torment.

"Well, I've gone through my options," he said, "and telling her she's not welcome in the class seems a little mean. Ignoring her hasn't worked, so being rude seems my best bet."

"Again, how's that working for you?" Jake teased.

"Exactly," Marcus groaned.

Jake turned the conversation back to Marcus's original concern. "You do know Marcus that there are stories in the Bible about men and women of God who were attracted to each other. It's not wrong to be attracted to her. And maybe, just a thought, it may be God's way of getting your attention."

"Oh, He's gotten my attention," Marcus laughed. "Of course, now it's about all I can think about."

"I know you, my friend," Jake said, "and I don't think there's a danger of you diving into an ungodly relationship based on a pretty face. The fact that we're having this conversation indicates you want to do His will."

"Tell me what you know about her."

"She's getting her Master of Fine Arts and graduates next week. She loves teaching children. Wicked sense of humor, quite intelligent but so free-spirited that she seems ditzy at times. Oh, and she's serious about her faith."

"Way to bury the lead, bud," Marcus said. "You knew I was asking about her spiritual life, but thanks for the bio. She needs to hire you as her public relations manager.

"My pleasure," Jake turned serious. "I will tell you this, Marcus. Carla and I like Rori. A lot. Don't go any deeper into this if you're not sure. I don't know the details, but I think something boy-related happened to her in high school. As delightful and pretty as she is, she has very little experience in relationships. You are my best friend but, I won't like it if you hurt her or break her heart."

"Understood," Marcus said. Jake's warning only echoed the one inside his own head.

Unwilling to act on his friend's advice without more debate, Marcus decided the only way to protect him, and Rori, was to adopt the veneer of indifference. He hoped she would realize it was a thinly veiled act, but he obviously did not know her well. Those closest to her would counsel him against such a tactic. Rori was such an open and carefree person that the thought of subterfuge of this sort, even for logical reasons, was outside of her understanding.

"I thought I did better last night," she said, bemoaning Chef MacRae's obvious irritation. "Why does he hate me so much?"

"At least he's not picking on you tonight," Jess pointed out. "He's just ignoring you."

"Exactly," Rori was meticulously chopping and slicing vegetables. They had been assigned Chinese cuisine tonight and were preparing their ingredients to put into the pressure cooker.

Almost every culinary region on the planet had a traditional meat dish combined with vegetables that was typically slow cooked. Marcus was introducing the students to the marvel of a pressure cooker that reduced the hours-long process to less than an hour. The class would be taking their quizzes while the stews cooked noisily on their stations.

"He really didn't like my slicing skills," Rori sulked, recalling the looks and sighs the chef leveled at her when he walked around the room during their preparation time. He stopped and helped several of the other students, all women she remembered, but at her station, he just shook his head and moved on.

"He didn't say anything," Jess reminded her.

"Not with his mouth." Rori continued her pout. "But with his eyes he did. I can't catch a break. I'm beginning to think I should just drop the class."

"No!" Jess insisted. "I'm going to make you stick it out. You need to be forced out of that dungeon, especially this week and next." Jess knew that pressure of the looming art show was only going to increase with each day. If her friend did not have something specific that required her out to leave the basement studio, Jess was afraid she was going to find Rori curled into a ball, unconscious from not eating or passed out from only breathing paint fumes.

Jess's exclamation was loud enough to attract attention, apparently, as Chef raised his eyebrow in inquiry.

"Everything all right, Your Highness?" Chef grimaced as he wished desperately that he could change his choice of words. I sound like a bully, he thought.

"Yes, Chef," the roommates answered in unison. Of course, with the tension of the evening so far, the singsong sound of their answer gave Rori a terrible case of the giggles. Chef's frown deepened, but he left them alone the rest of the evening.

The stews were delicious and those in the class that had never seen—much less used—a pressure cooker, were congratulating themselves. The Spanish stew that an older couple who were taking the class for fun was Rori's favorite.

John Liu insisted the Chinese red stew she and Jess had prepared was the best, and it did in fact garner a nod and 'Not bad,' from Chef Marcus. Or Chef high-and-mighty-Marcus, as Rori was referring to him in her mind by the end of the evening. It was starting to irk her that he singled her out for either pointed criticism or total ignoring. There was no in-between. She was starting to think she had imagined their secret email conversations.

"Well, three down, nine to go," the weary artist sighed as she and Jess left the building. Her roommate had insisted that she not go back to the studio tonight.

"God will take care of you getting your pieces done," Jess had encouraged her. She added playfully, "If you need help, I can always throw something together, too. It'll be great! Everyone will say, 'Wow I love Aurora's work, except that one piece that looks like a two-year-old did it!'"

"That would probably be their favorite piece," Rori moped.

"That attitude is exactly why you will not be going back to the studio tonight," the roommate turned dictator insisted. "Ice cream and coffee, it is!" Calling out to their classmates, "Hey, John and Calvin, come with us. We're going to go drown our sorrows in coffee and ice cream."

"I will gladly come to your rescue, Princesses," John bowed deeply, his mysterious Asian eyes twinkling. "How ever I may assist you, I am yours to command."

John's friend, Calvin, who was one of the college's most promising wrestlers, swept a deep bow alongside his friend. Slated to try out for the Olympics this summer, he knew his size intimidated many of their classmates. Rori and Jess had both had him in several classes, so they knew he was in fact just a big softie.

The girls laughed and each took the arm of one of the knights-in-shining armor and headed for the café across from the main campus boulevard. The tall red headed man observing their interplay turned and slammed the lesson plans on the desk in his office. Papers scattered, leaving the office in a state that matched his mood.

"Jake," Marcus held his head in his hands and spoke into the phone. "I need help. I know it's late, but can I come by and talk to you and Carla?"

"No problem, bud," Jake could hear the exhaustion in his friend's voice. "Kiddo's asleep and coffee's on."

"I don't know why she gets under my skin," Marcus leaned his head back in the comfortable overstuffed chairs in the Hampton's den. He missed the secret smile between the young couple.

After Jake visited the class the day before, they had discussed the situation at length. Instead of laying their theory out to him, though, the young couple wanted

Marcus to come to his own conclusions. It may be more painful this way, but Jake wanted the realization to be internal. He knew from experience that being forced into a relationship just because everyone around said, 'Oh you make a cute couple,' could be a big mistake. Carla agreed that Rori was a perfect match for Marcus, but neither she nor Jake wanted to get in front of God's will and guidance. *Patience,* they had both decided.

"I find myself being purposefully mean to her," Marcus agonized, "but I can't seem to help myself."

"Tell you what," Jake offered, "I'll come help teach tomorrow night. It's pasta night anyway, right? We both know my pasta making skills are far, far superior to yours, what with the Italian heritage and all."

"What good will that do?" Marcus was thinking that was the worst idea ever. Having his best friend observe his terrible behavior towards this lovely young lady would only mean he would have to endure chastisement for hours afterwards.

"That will allow you to ignore her," Jake explained. "I'll do the demonstration and then we can split up the class for closer interaction. You just be sure to take the opposite side of the room."

"That might work," Marcus reluctantly admitted, now inexplicably a little ticked at his friend. He was more upset with himself for the feeling of jealously that came from watching his best friend would be working with Aurora.

"Better?" Jake asked his friend pointedly as he prepared to leave.

"Yes, thanks," Marcus said. Calling into the kitchen, "Thanks, Carla for the goodies. Kiss that Princess Zoe for me." Princess. That seems to be a recurring theme in my life lately. He groaned as he headed to his car.

Resolved to do this, she forced herself to sit in front of her computer and turn it on. Maybe he would get so mad at her request that he would ask her to drop the class. Tomorrow at noon was the deadline to receive a full refund. After that, she was out any money she paid for tuition, plus a failing grade would go on her transcript. She was taking it for credit thinking it would help round out her resume.

Dear Chef: (she refused still to call him Marcus) *I was wondering what the class policy was for absences? I have an art show a week from Saturday night, but the art professors have just scheduled a preview cocktail hour on Friday evening. I know this is sort of last minute, but if there is any way I can be excused from class that night, I would be grateful. I checked the syllabus and it looks like we are doing the second half of the group presentations on Friday night. If Miss Johnston and I could do ours on Thursday, then it would not hurt her grade for me to be gone on Friday. Although she would do better without me, I am sure you would agree. Thank you. ~Aurora Sinclair.*

She hit the send button nervously. All he could do is say no, right? Or, she thought, he could say no and hold it against you.

Shocked to see her name in his inbox, he selected her message. He read it twice, took a deep breath, and read it again. She hates me (why else would she want to miss class), she thinks I'm a brute (he could hear her saying, 'I am sure you would agree'), and we've slipped back into Aurora Sinclair instead of just Aurora. And did she think I was joking about the Marcus instead of Chef Marcus?

Blinded with frustration, and completely forgetting the resolutions he had made while talking with Jake and Carla, he quickly typed:

Dear Miss Sinclair: Your class attendance is entirely a personal decision. If you decide it's important to miss next Friday, please be sure to sign up for one of the Thursday demonstration slots. ~Chef MacRae

5
Perfect Portraits

Carla answered the knock at her door, surprised to see her good friend. "Hey, Rori. Shouldn't you be toiling away in the studio?"

"I'm waiting for one of my paintings to dry before I can finish the next layer," the young painter replied. "So, the whole 'watching paint dry' isn't just a cliché?" Carla laughed. "Come in. You can help keep Zoe occupied while I make lunch."

"Aunt Wa-Ree!" Zoe skipped down the hall.

"Hey, squirt!" Rori twirled the four-year-old around. "Let's draw something while Mommy cooks us a delicious lunch."

"I wanna draw you!" Zoe plopped down at the kitchen table where her crayons and a pad of construction paper were spread in lovely, creative disarray.

"Okay, Zoe," Rori agreed, "and I'll draw you." The real reason Rori had stopped by was to ask Carla about Chef MacRae. As far as she knew, no one since high school had ever instantly disliked her and Rori was curious as to what she had done to make him hate her. His last email made his feelings, or indifference, clear.

"So, Rori," Carla asked as she sliced homemade bread for grilled cheese sandwiches, "how's your cooking class going? Is Marcus treating you well?" Carla was brimming with curiosity ever since Marcus had admitted that he was attracted to Rori. *At least I know that's true, even if he is having a hard time admitting it,* Carla thought.

"Ha," Rori guffawed, "I wish. I think he hates me. I can't seem to do anything right and I have such a hard time being serious for very long that my humor always seems to come out at the wrong times. Is he always so serious?"

"No, actually, he's really a kind person," Carla wanted to give her friend the most complete picture of Marcus that she could.

"Really?" Rori mumbled. "Could have fooled me."

"Stop frowning, Aunt Wa-Ree!" Zoe was taking her portrait drawing very seriously.

Carla laughed at her intense daughter's comment. "Yes, Rori, stop frowning. Marcus is Jake's best friend, and I would think you know us well enough that you could trust our judgment."

"Point taken," Rori admitted, casually sketching the youngster sitting across from her. "So, tell me about this 'prince' of a man." Carla was amazed that Rori could hold a serious conversation and draw so beautifully at the same time.

"Marcus grew up in a good, faithful family, although they are quite a bit more reserved than your family probably is. I think it's something in his mom's proper British upbringing and all. He has a younger brother

Collin, a younger sister named Katie, and an older brother, James who's married and has a son about Zoe's age."

"Nice cookbook cover information," Rori said wryly, "but I'd like something juicier, please."

"Juicier?" Carla laughed. "Like is he dating someone? Does he like brunettes or redheads? Is he a secret agent or in witness protection?"

"Is he?" Rori stopped sketching long enough to look intently at Carla. The serious look in Rori's eyes let the young mom know just how deeply her husband's friend had affected her. But she had to be sure.

"Is he what?" Carla asked teasingly.

"Dating anyone?" Rori ventured.

"No. He dated a little in college from what I can remember, but not a lot since then. His standards are high, thankfully. He loves Zoe and his nephew, and from what we see, both Jake and I think he'll make a marvelous father." Carla decided to press for some answers. "Why the sudden interest?"

"I don't know," Rori said. "I've tried to figure that out myself. I think it just may be that he doesn't seem to like me and I want to figure out why." She seemed truly unsure of her own motivations, so Carla backed off even though she suspected there was more to Rori's motivation.

"What else do you want to know?" Carla asked.

"What did he do after culinary school?" Rori was now completely focused on her adult conversation, and Zoe was coloring in her picture so her inattention was accepted.

"He took a job as chef at a fancy ski resort, which seemed unusual at the time," Carla explained. "He was close to the top of their graduating class, so the position he took was not as prestigious as expected. But we found out later that his mom was caring for his step-grandmother who was suffering from Alzheimer's disease. The assisted living complex was a couple hours away from the resort, so it was a perfect chance for him to help out."

Rori was quietly trying to take all this in. Marcus was not what he appeared to be on the surface.

"I know you don't know all of our history, either, but Marcus played a big role in getting me and Jake together, too."

"Really?" So, Chef Charming is a matchmaker, too, Rori thought.

"Yes," Carla was obviously revisiting the time in her memories. "Jake went through a tough time when he lost his dad and wouldn't have made it without Marcus. Jake had turned into a hotheaded ruffian. Marcus's prayers and friendship were what brought him out of that dark time. It was right after that that he introduced me to Jake."

Rori was quiet. There was really nothing she could say. Carla set the plate of lunchmeat and cheese out. They were going to have gourmet grilled cheese sandwiches, apparently. Rori just then noticed how much food was on the platter.

"Expecting company?" Rori asked at the same time she heard the front door open. Marcus followed Jake into the kitchen. He was startled to see her sitting at Carla's kitchen table.

"Aurora?" The chef's surprise and embarrassment were evident in his voice. He and Jake had just spent an hour playing racquetball. It was a twice-weekly routine they had started in college and resumed when Marcus came on staff in the spring. Only Jake saw the look of panic.

"Hey, Rori!" Jake said as he hugged his wife and planted a wet kiss on her cheek.

"Ew, you're sweaty and stinky!" Carla laughed and dodged a second attempt for a kiss from her husband.

"I know, I know," Jake tweaked Zoe's nose after releasing his wife, "but you'll have to wait. I promised Marcus he could change here since you were preparing your famous gourmet grilled cheese sandwiches. I tried to lie to him and say we wouldn't have enough for his wolf-like appetite." What Rori did not know was this was a pure spur of the moment fabrication. Marcus threw him a look of gratitude as he headed for the master bedroom to clean up and change clothes.

Jake spent the few minutes it took his friend to change admiring his daughter's masterpiece. And Rori's, of course.

"Zoe drew me and I drew her," Rori explained.

"Ah, that helps," Jake nodded. "I could tell this was you," he said to Rori as he pointed to Zoe's childlike depiction, "but I'm glad you told me yours was supposed to be Zoe."

"Daddy, that is not nice," Zoe reprimanded her father. "Aunt Wa-ree tried her very best. And she likes to draw, which is the most important thing. Right?" Her last question was directed at her art teacher.

"Yes, Zoe," Rori loved the interplay with this sweet girl. "You are absolutely right. Art is about enjoying yourself."

"A lot like cooking," a familiar voice came from the hallway.

How long had he been standing there? And couldn't he try a little harder to be less handsome? Rori's thoughts raced.

"My turn to get all prettified," Jake declared as he pushed away from the kitchen table. He threw Marcus a loaded look and decided to push some buttons.

"Marcus, Zoe and Rori just drew lovely pictures of each other," he said, adding mischievously, "maybe they could draw you next." Marcus threw him an 'I'm going to get you for this' look.

"No," Rori said at the same time Zoe exclaimed, "Yes! Yes! I want to draw Uncle Marcus!"

"I need to get back to the studio," Rori pleaded.

"Not before you eat!" Carla insisted.

"Scared?" Marcus said quietly as he leaned over to admire her portrait of Zoe. He couldn't seem to resist inciting her. It was patently obvious she did not wish to be in the same room with him.

"Of you?" The words were out of her mouth before she thought.

"Are you?" he retorted.

"No," she came back.

"Prove it." He sat on the stool at the kitchen counter and folded his arms, striking a pose ready for his portrait.

"Fine," Rori conceded, unable to keep a touch of annoyance from her voice. "Let's draw Uncle Marcus, Zoe. Do you want to use the crayons or should I?" She couldn't resist the comment, letting him know she thought he was being childish.

"Me," Zoe volunteered. "I like all the colors."

Rori was determined to get the torture over with quickly. She sketched Marcus, arms folded, holding a curved knife in one hand and a cooking whisk in the other. She grinned at the image. She added a plaid sash across his muscular chest, trying to ignore the broad shoulders, chiseled features, and gorgeous auburn hair.

"Do you have a specific clan tartan for your family?" Her question surprised him. Not everyone knew of the Scottish heritage of plaids. "I can borrow Zoe's crayons to make this more authentic."

"Blue and green, mainly," Marcus replied succinctly, squirming under the intense attention from Rori.

"Zoe, may I borrow your crayons? Just blue and green, please." Rori picked out the necessary colors after the little girl nodded. Minutes later, she turned over her sketchbook and stood up.

"I'm done," Rori stated, and thanked Carla for the sandwich she had eaten while she was sketching. "I've got to get back to the studio." Looking at Zoe's depiction of Marcus, she complimented the young artist.

"You've done a marvelous job, Zoe! That smile is definitely Uncle Marcus."

"Are you not going to share your masterpiece, Miss Sinclair?" Marcus had moved into the kitchen to create his grilled cheese from the array of ingredients. Although he tried to make his tone sound uninterested, he was very anxious to see her artwork.

"I'll leave it, but will need to take my sketchbook," Rori tore the page out and placed it face down on the counter.

"Aren't you going to autograph it?" Marcus asked.

"Already did," she smiled a falsely sweet smile. She tried to send him a message, *I know you're trying to annoy me, but it's not going to work.*

As she closed the door, he turned over the paper. She had drawn him with a fierce, warrior-like look. It was uncannily good. Her choice of weapons was comical. He couldn't help but laugh.

"Oh, she's good," Marcus said, his tone making it clear that he referred to more than just her artistic skill. *She knows exactly what to do to provoke me.*

"What was she doing here?" he asked Carla. "Isn't she neck deep in completing her art work for her show or something?"

Carla shrugged her shoulders, dismissing the importance of her conversation with Rori. She was not going to tell Marcus that he was the topic of their talk until after she talked to Jake about it.

"She said she was waiting for one of her pieces to dry before she could complete it," Jake's wife explained. "And we're friends, remember?"

"Whatever," Marcus mumbled.

"He has it bad, honey," Jake badgered his friend. "We should take it easy on him. Poor guy."

"I'm outta here," Marcus finished his sandwich, and kissed Zoe on the tip of her nose, thanking her for her lovely artwork, which he promised to put on his fridge.

Jake walked him to the door.

"Really, Marcus," he said, "if you need to talk, let me know."

"I will."

Jake returned to his wife. "Spill it," he said. Carla described her conversation with Rori.

"So, Rori likes Marcus and Marcus likes Rori," Jake summarized his wife's take on the situation.

"This is not junior high school, dear," Carla poked him. "This is serious."

"I know, I know," Jake said. "She's scheduled to move right after graduation, so we need to work fast!"

6
Perplexing Pasta

Rori purposefully slipped into class right before starting time. Being late would bring unwanted attention but she did not want to risk being alone with Marcus before class either. She had not returned to the studio after lunch at the Hamptons, but instead had stopped by the church to talk to the assistant pastor.

Reverend Samuel Collins had been on the retreat where Rori had first gotten to know Jake and Carla well, and he thought this lovely young lady was a delight. To see her so distressed concerned him.

"I've never had anyone take me in dislike so quickly," Rori shared with the young pastor. "I know it shouldn't surprise me, and in the long run shouldn't really matter, but am I doing something wrong? I don't want to irritate the man to the point of frustration."

"Why shouldn't it surprise you that someone might dislike you?" Her statement confused Sam. He couldn't imagine anyone disliking Rori Sinclair. She was one of the friendliest and most lighthearted people he knew. Of course, he knew that the carefree attitude could be a defense mechanism. He would address this later if he needed to.

Not wanting to delve into a painful memory from her past, she tried to downplay her comment. Rori became quiet, feelings from high school flooding in. Sam noticed her hesitation, though.

"I'm so unruly and messy compared to him," Rori said, choosing to stick with to current problem.

"I think there's more to it, Rori," Sam pressed. "If you are really concerned about dealing with Marcus MacRae, you're going to need to be completely honest with me, and with yourself."

"There was a guy in high school that treated me pretty badly," Rori didn't want to dwell on the incident so summarized it, hoping to convey that she had dealt with it and moved on. "I was a wreck for a few months, but he met with me and my parents a couple years later and apologized. I think I had pretty much forgotten about it until this week. Even though I'm over it, I know it made me leery where guys are involved."

"I see how that could affect your perception of Chef MacRae's attitude towards you," the pastor agreed. "Tell me a little more about your interaction with him."

"Are you by chance attracted to this man?" Sam asked after listening attentively to her take on the situation. He had suspicions about what was really going on, both on Rori's part and probably also on Chef MacRae's side.

She was not at all prepared for the question.

"What does the fact that he is good-looking have to do with anything?" she asked, a tad defensively.

"So, you do find him attractive?" The young pastor asked, barely hiding a smile.

"I didn't say that," Rori protested, albeit a bit lamely. "Even if I did, I still don't see what that has to do with anything." She was not willing to admit outright how Marcus made her feel.

"Well," the young pastor continued. "I think we talk so much about the dangers of infatuation that we forget that God created physical attraction, too. While it is dangerous, and I'd even say very dangerous, to base a relationship solely or primarily on physical features, many of us would have never found the one God had for us if they hadn't 'turned our heads' so to speak the first time we met them."

Aurora sat in silence, struggling to adjust her thinking. This was out of left field, she thought, and I don't even like baseball, her silliness snuck in.

"Did you stop to think that it was not coincidence that you took his class?" Sam asked. "I'm not saying God has grave plans for you to reform this hardened, bitter man, but I hear confusion as well as frustration in your voice. I think you actually like this man, despite his harshness toward you."

"But he hates me," Rori blurted.

"I doubt that," Pastor Collins cautioned her. "But even if he did, it doesn't change the fact that God placed you in his class for a reason. You'll need to determine what that reason is. Maybe it's to teach him to be more patient, or to teach you that there are going to be unpleasant people in your life."

Not sure which theory she liked best – she was the problem or Marcus was. Either she needed to be nice to him because God was teaching her patience, or Marcus was the one with the problem and her presence in his class was meant to irritate him into showing patience himself.

"Or," Pastor broke into her thoughts, "It could be like I said before, an attraction that you will have to determine is either infatuation or something deeper."

That theory is pure nonsense, Rori thought. She tried to ignore her heartbeat's response to the idea.

"Either way, I'll be praying for you, starting now." The young pastor, himself a newlywed, took her hands and prayed, "Father, please guide this lovely young lady in the path you have for her. I know she is confused and unsure of her feelings towards this man, but you are not a God of confusion. Help her seek Your will and make Your path clear to her. Amen."

"Thanks, Sam," Rori stood and shook out her long jeans skirt. "I promise to spend some time in prayer before class, examining my attitude. I appreciate you letting me talk through this. Despite the teacher, I am really enjoying the class, and maybe I'll learn enough to make you and Ruthie a gourmet meal."

"Sounds delicious," Sam walked her to the door. "What's the topic tonight?"

"Pasta," Rori shuddered. "Yikes."

"Yum," Sam laughed.

Jake smoothly took over the teaching duties that evening. He was correct in his assessment of his superior pasta skills, although Marcus would never admit it.

Mastering the delicacy of working the dough was difficult for several of the students, but for some reason Rori caught on immediately. Perhaps it was her artist's control of her hands, or more likely the lack of pressure from having Marcus ready to pounce on her every misstep.

"Very nice, Rori," Jake praised her. "Are you sure you're not part Italian?"

"You're so right," Rori admittedly mischievously. "What gave it away? Was it my blonde hair or the blue eyes?"

Marcus cringed at the sound of his friend's laughter. He knew without turning around that Jake was working at Jess and Rori's table right now. This was what he wanted for tonight, so why did the good-natured camaraderie irk him so much? He would have been even more upset had he overheard their conversation.

"So, you and Marcus are best buddies, I see," Jake teased her.

"Not sure that's what I'd call it," she answered wryly. "We just seem to be destined to annoy each other."

"You guys are as different as night and day in some ways," Jake said, "but bizarrely similar in others."

"No way," Rori laughed. "Like how?"

"You have the same sense of humor," Jake told her.

"Chef MacRae has a sense of humor?" she asked incredulously.

"Exactly." Jake laughed loudly, eliciting a glare from across the room. He returned to his instructor duties with a grin on his face, convinced that his friend should pursue this delightful young lady. It would do Marcus good to have someone shake up his ordered world.

He and Jake had prepared several sauces for the class to choose from for their pastas. The skill of making, rolling, and shaping the pastas would fill the two-hour class time, so they opted to do the sauces and filings themselves. Only two of the groups were doing filled pastas, so Jake had shown them individually how to prepare simple and quick fillings. Of course, Jess had chosen a filled version for the challenge, giving Jake more time with Aurora.

Marcus finished up with his last group and then returned to his station to make sure the sauces were ready. The pasta would cook quickly, so he was waiting until everyone had ample time for instruction and feedback.

"Okay, class," Jake rejoined Marcus in the center of the lab, "If your water is boiling sufficiently, go ahead and drop in your pasta. Fresh pasta cooks very quickly, so keep an eye on it, paying attention to the details we gave you."

"How you doin'?" Jake turned to Marcus using his best New Jersey shore accent.

Marcus just growled at him.

"Down, boy," his friend laughed. "This little 'ignore it and it will go away' experiment - not so successful, huh?"

"You seemed to be enjoying it," Marcus glowered at him, his jealousy giving a critical, almost accusatory, tone to his words.

"If this weren't so funny, I'd knock you out for that one, buddy," Jake was exasperated with Marcus. "You have a distinct green hue about your entire being right now. Perhaps you need to see a doctor." He walked away from Marcus before he said anything he would regret later. He remembered how it felt when he first met Carla and how totally ticked off he became at the charming fraternity boy that hung around her all the time. That is, until he found out frat boy was her cousin.

"All right class," the visiting chef called for their attention. "Most of your pastas should be done. Get them out of the pot and ready to serve. It smells delicious in here!"

The dishes were in fact very delicious. Rori was so proud of herself for having conquered the difficult skill that she resolved to not let the ill-mannered chef affect her mood. I can survive this, especially if the benefits include eating like this every night.

Ignoring the fact that she could easily research the question online, she drafted an email to Marcus. It was an irresistible addiction. She sat in front of the computer screen vowing not to reach out to her nemesis, but it was if her fingers had a mind of their own. She chuckled to herself and made a mental note to sketch her hand with faces on each of her fingers.

Dear Chef Charming… Nope, better not go there…

Dear Chef: Could you settle an argument, well not really an argument, more of a disagreement... no really it was just a discussion… Is all Italian food the same or is there a difference in regions? I thought I remembered hearing about two regions…North and south, or east and west… not sure, but John, Calvin, and I were talking about it and they think I'm crazy. Jess wouldn't settle it for us, because, well, I promised not to tell so never mind why she wouldn't help us. Am I right? Please, please, I hope so. The guys were so smug! Thanks! Aurora

He could hear her voice in his head. Some would call her rambling flighty. He found it intoxicating. Following her thought pattern was like a roller coaster ride. The mention of the two young men that he was sorely tempted to flunk brought a slight frown to his face. At least she's still willing to talk to me, even if it's only via computer. He decided he'd best make the most of the opportunity.

Dear Aurora: He paused. This was the first time he had ventured to use her first name. In his mind she was always 'Princess Aurora.' Deciding Aurora was preferable to not the nickname Rori that everyone else seemed to love, or the more formal 'Miss Sinclair,' he continued.

I am happy to oblige. Yes, you are very correct. The terrain in the Northern part of Italy is quite different from the Southern lands, and therefore two distinct cuisine styles have emerged. The Northern region is most like France, its neighbor, and the Southern region is more like what an American would think of as Italian food. But even within these two divisions, there are smaller regions with their own distinct characteristics. This would be a great choice for you and Miss Johnston for your final project. I would be glad to assist in any way. ~Marcus.

He hesitated, considering deleting his last sentence. In his head he heard Jake say, "Suck it up, big guy, and go for it!" He hit the send button before he changed his mind.

8
A Slice of Quiche

Marcus felt like a spy. He was determined to locate the mysterious art studio where Aurora spent much of her time. He had already stopped by the after-school program and glanced in to make sure she was teaching today. That way he could scope out the dungeon, as Miss Johnston termed it, without the danger of running into Rori.

He could smell the paint fumes and hear the music as he got closer. He hesitated. *Great plan Sherlock, what are you going to do now? Step inside and say 'I'm stalking one of your students, could you please show me her work?'*

Before he could decide on advancing or retreating, the head of the art department who was also the professor in charge of the seniors and graduate school students stepped out of his office, almost colliding with Marcus.

"Professor Smith," Marcus offered his hand. "We met at the incoming staff orientation a couple months ago."

"Yes, Chef MacRae, isn't it?" Rori's favorite art instructor asked. "What can I do for you, sir? We don't normally see the culinary staff down here in the basement unless they're lost."

"No, this was an intentional foray," Marcus laughed. Quick, think of something!

"Perhaps you need an illustrator for a cookbook, or a piece of abstract art featuring large tomatoes and cucumbers for your new digs?" Professor Smith had an outrageous sense of humor, which was endearing to some and annoying to others.

Thank you, Lord! Marcus breathed silently.

"As a matter of fact," Marcus latched onto the lifeline the art teacher threw out, "Professor Hampton suggested we compile a cook book each year from favorite recipes of our students. It wouldn't necessarily be anything fancy, but I think some nice, simple illustrations would add a unique touch."

"Well, the seniors and grad students are up to their eyeballs in work because of the big art show next weekend, but I will think about who might be a good fit. What's the timeline on it?"

"Oh, we're just in the thinking stages right now." Thankfully, this was not a lie since Jake did in fact mention this once, a long time ago. It was a very long time ago—like six years ago in culinary school.

"Perfect." The art instructor walked back down the hall with Marcus, "you should come to the art show. I think one of my most promising students is in your evening class."

"Oh, really?" Marcus feigned surprise.

"Yes," Dr. Smith continued, "Rori Sinclair. It's Aurora Sinclair, but most people call her Rori or

Princess, which I assume is a reference to some fairy tale." The elderly widower must not have a young granddaughter, Marcus thought.

"Yes," Marcus answered, "Aurora is in my class. I appreciate you considering the illustrations, but again, there's no hurry." He couldn't really think of anything else to say, afraid to give away a hint of his real level of interest in the young lady.

"Would you like to look around the studio at the pieces in progress?"

The professor's offer terrified and thrilled Marcus at the same time. "I wouldn't want to disturb any of the artists," Marcus stammered. He knew Rori wasn't in the studio but wasn't sure he wanted any of her compatriots to know of his interest.

"Oh, no one's in the studio right now. Most of them are at lunch, except for Rori," Dr. Smith explained. "She's teaching upstairs. Even if they were here, though, artists always welcome an excuse to take a break and talk about their masterpieces."

As they moved through the chaotic art space, Marcus smiled at the similarity between Rori's kitchen area during class and the disarray of most of the art student's areas. As he looked around, he spotted Rori's work immediately. Although he had just met the young woman, he felt such a deep connection to her already that her pieces seemed to scream for his attention.

The professor was pointing out various works around the studio, but Marcus focused on Rori's work, which was nestled in the far corner. He did not hide his distraction well enough, though, and the professor wisely led the way to Rori's area. It was obvious to the older man that the young chef was smitten. Dr. Smith smiled to himself. It was also obvious that Mr. MacRae was trying desperately to hide his interest. Ever the romantic, the art professor decided to help the young man.

"Rori's work in particular is quite interesting," Professor Smith said, "especially for those who don't know the delightful young lady very well. Some of it is already wrapped up for transport to the gallery, but there are enough her to give you a sense of her style. It is quite eclectic. She seems fall in love with every new technique she tries."

Marcus was stunned. The paintings ranged from large vibrant, abstract landscapes, to smaller, strangely calming watercolors. They seemed to mirror perfectly what little he knew of this fascinating woman. In her works he saw the lively Rori he saw in class that railed against his instruction and drove him to the point of frustration and the contrite, playful Rori he conversed with each night. As he stared at her work, a smaller piece caught his eye.

"This one looks quite different from the others. Is this going to be part of the show?" The title of the piece made him smile.

"She did that one afternoon, on a whim, apparently," Dr. Smith said. "It is quite haunting at first glance, but the more you look at it, the more a sense of hope comes over you. I find it fascinating. Rori doesn't want to sell it for some reason. I think it holds some sort of meaning to her."

"Fascinating," Marcus said quietly. *Aurora's Castle.* Haunting was a good description. An overwhelming desire to find a coat of armor and a white stallion popped into his mind. Realizing that he may not be able to hide his feelings much longer from the astute professor, Marcus moved on to some of the other students' work, hoping his questions did not sound as insincere as they felt. Being so close to what was obviously an extremely personal space for her was making it hard for Marcus to think of anything but Rori.

"Thank you, Dr. Smith," Marcus finally said, hiding his panic as he heard students in the hallway. "I appreciate the tour. I'll get back to you on the other matter."

"Certainly," Dr. Smith said. Trying to better gauge the level of interest, he added, "I think you would really enjoy the art show, too. Many of the pieces will be available for purchase, too, if you've seen anything you like here. It's at five o'clock next Saturday at the downtown art gallery. Hope to see you there." Dr. Smith couldn't help but laugh at the hasty retreat the chef made. Too bad Rori wasn't in the group of artists Marcus passed as he fled the scene. That would have been an interchange worth witnessing.

As the students entered the building that evening, they were once again greeted with the marvelous aroma of bacon. The topic of tonight's class was quiche. Marcus was hoping to teach them all the art of a perfect piecrust and have them hone their cutting and mixing skills on the relatively easy recipes. He was not of the chauvinist opinion that real men don't eat quiche.

The fabulous foursome as Marcus thought of Rori, Jessica, and the two young men stalking them, arrived together, laughing at some inside joke. The instructor had never taken two students in such dislike before. Hopefully John and Calvin did not sense his annoyance.

"Tonight, class, we will be making quiche," Marcus began. "This will entail mastering a perfect piecrust, which, if you follow the instructions carefully, can be done, I promise!" He tried to keep his tone light, hoping that pretending to be in a good mood would translate itself into actuality.

Glancing over at Aurora and Jess's table, he saw her dramatically rub her stomach. He completely lost his train of thought. She's an enchantress. Stay away! His mind warned him. He could almost hear Jake's voice laughing at him.

"We'll begin with a piecrust demonstration and then you will find eight different recipes and the ingredients for each of the fillings, here at my station. You may come and choose which to make. Each one will involve some practice with your knife skills, and I'll be coming around to check on your progress."

For the piecrust instruction, the class gathered around John and Calvin's station, because it was the biggest of the student areas. Chef carefully showed them the steps to mixing the flour, butter, and water, and how to delicately roll out the dough. Each partnership would make two pies and the crusts would chill in the refrigerators while they prepared the fillings.

Making piecrusts was a skill that didn't worry Rori. Even Jess agreed that she made a marvelous apple pie. The roommates decided to each make one of the crusts and were placing their creations in the refrigerator when Chef told the class they should be completing their crusts and should move on to the quiche fillings.

Rori and Jess had chosen a quiche Lorraine recipe and had gathered their ingredients. Hoping to avoid being scrutinized by Marcus over her cutting skills, Rori chopped her chives and bacon first. She glanced at the chef out of the corner of her eye and realized he had started his inspections on the other side of the class.

"I'm sure he started over there on purpose, so he can save my awesome skills for last," she whispered to Jess, who couldn't hold back her bark of laughter. Marcus glanced at the pair and raised a suspicious eyebrow.

Because this was such an important evaluation time, it did in fact take the chef most the class time to get to their side of the room. By then many of the groups were removing their cooked quiches from the oven. He ended his evaluations two stations away from them with the Watkins, an older couple who were taking the class purely for enjoyment. Since their vegetable quiche was already baking, he asked the pair to chop a carrot so he could evaluate their skills, praising both for their progress.

"All right, class," Chef announced, "that evaluation took longer than expected. If your quiches are ready, please cut a piece and I'll come around and give you some feedback. Those that did not get to show me your improved knife skills, I will get to later." He looked pointedly at Jess and Aurora.

"Anyone else that wants to taste the creations may do so, too," he added as he cut a piece of John and Calvin's quiche. He scribbled some notes in the grade book and nodded to the two young men. "Flaky crust, vegetables cooked well. You might consider a little more salt next time, but overall, quite nice."

His evaluations of the next few quiches were similar. Each pair was able to take any leftover quiches with them and leave when Chef finished tasting theirs, but most everyone stayed so they could try all the delicious creations.

Only three groups' quiches were left to be tasted when he moved to Aurora and Jess. They had already cut a piece for him and placed it neatly on a plate. Aurora remembered hearing, "You eat with your eyes first," and being an artist, this statement made perfect sense to her. She had taken special care to cut a neat piece and had added a garnish of a couple of green onion sprigs.

"Nice presentation," Marcus noted. "You two ladies did not get to show me your knife skills, but it looks like

65

these ingredients were cut by a pro," Marcus tried to keep his tone upbeat.

Thinking to make a joke, he continued, "Are you sure, Miss Sinclair, that Miss Johnston didn't do all the work here?"

Her exhaustion from the studio hours she was keeping, and the fact that he seemed determined to dislike her, set the normally cheerful coed on edge.

"Excuse me?" she blurted. "I will have you know I did *all* the chopping for this recipe, thank you very much."

"Prove it," he snapped as his frustration over his reaction to this woman won over his determination to remain calm and pleasant. He could always blame it on his Scottish ancestry---that, and the stereotypical redheaded temperament. He grabbed a carrot and slammed it on her cutting board.

Thankfully, the rest of the class had decided this was a perfect time to clean up their stations and quietly moved away from the clash of personalities playing out before them.

Rori's hands were shaking with anger and she attempted to finely dice half the carrot and julienne the other half.

"Ouch!" she cried as the knife slipped and blood appeared on the end of her ring finger. Thankfully, it was not her left hand, which would have greatly hampered her next few days in the studio.

Chef leapt into action, as did Jess, who grabbed their first aid kit. Each station in the classroom was equipped with one, since such accidents were quite common occurrences in beginning cooking classes.

Marcus grabbed Rori's hand and thrust it under the faucet, running cold water over the cut.

"You fool," he sputtered. What Rori did not know was that he was speaking to himself, not to her. He foolishly let his frustration over his feelings for this young lady put her in danger.

As Jess held out the bandage for him after he dried off Rori's finger, she asked Marcus quietly, "Do you want me to release the rest of the class?"

"Yes, please," he nodded in gratitude. "Have those that I have not evaluated leave me two pieces of quiche and a piece of paper with their email address. I'll taste them and send them feedback tonight."

Jess relayed these instructions to the class, and added "Don't worry about cleaning up, we'll take care of it." In response to John and Calvin's concern, she assured them that Rori was fine.

"She'll be okay. She's just mad at herself and no, it's not her drawing hand, thank goodness."

Aurora's heart was beating wildly. It wasn't from the pain in her finger, she reluctantly admitted. It was from the closeness of this man. How could someone infuriate her and fascinate her at the same time? She could smell his aftershave and hear his breathing as he practically manhandled her in his effort to make up for her clumsiness.

"You two unfortunately will have to stay to help me tonight," Marcus broke the news to them as he dried his hands and wiped up the tiny spots of blood on Rori's station. Thankfully, no blood had gotten on their quiche. "As you know part of the class is learning to evaluate and critique gourmet food, so tonight you two will get your turn."

"Then we'll help clean up," Jess added. "I told the class they could go without finishing their stations. I thought it was more important to get them out of here."

"That's fine, but unnecessary," Chef didn't think he could stand to watch Aurora do such a patently domestic task as cleaning up several kitchens. Watching her with the children this afternoon had been difficult enough.

"It's the least I can do," Rori said quietly. Jess watched her roommate with concern. Rori's feelings for this man were evident to her, and she knew that tonight's incident had rattled her sensitive friend. Jess also had suspicions about Marcus after watching him watch Rori each night during class.

Chef moved to the first station that had quiches left for evaluation. There were two plates and two forks. Without thinking, he handed one fork to Jess, and with the other fed a bite to Aurora and then took one himself. The intimacy of the gesture made Jess's eyes widen. They have no idea that they are completely and utterly infatuated with each other, Jess realized.

Marcus walked them through the process of evaluating the crust and uniformity of the ingredients as well as the overall taste and texture of the quiche. He was thankful that both Miss Johnston and Aurora were able to give him good, insightful feedback. As a bonus, the Princess didn't like John and Calvin's quiche at all.

Since the pair insisted on cleaning up the food lab, Marcus provided Aurora with a glove to cover her injury. He busied himself at his station and in his office. Low murmurs replaced their typically cheerful chatter. He missed the craziness that usually surrounded the genie that haunted his life.

"Thank you, ladies," Chef finally dismissed them. "I'll finish up. It is getting late. Don't forget tomorrow's class is early since it is Saturday. We are doing breads, both yeast and quick, so it will take our entire three hours."

They collected their things and headed for the door. Aurora stopped as she heard him call her name.

"Miss Sinclair, you're going to be all right, yes?" He seemed to be asking and demanding at the same time.

"Yes, Chef." Rori answered, enigmatically as well. "I think so."

Are you sure you're okay? The words on her phone blinked at her. His text arrived less than ten minutes later, just as she and Jess got home. Her roommate had refused to let her go to the studio.

Yes, thank you for asking. You were right to call me foolish. I will try to do better and not bother you so much.

Since he had been staring at his phone, willing her to respond, he received her response as she sent it. He groaned, realizing the damage he had done, not only physically, but also emotionally.

My 'Fool' comment was directed at myself. I should never have let my frustration put you in such a position. I am sorry.

I'm sorry I am so much trouble. She responded.

If you only knew, Marcus wanted to reply. Instead, he just sent a quick, *Goodnight, Aurora.*

Goodnight, Marcus.

9
Bread of Strife

Kneading the dough with a bandaged finger was not an easy task. At least she could be grateful that Marcus was avoiding her today. The only time she recalled seeing him look at her was when she and John accidently created a cloud of flour that engulfed the two of them. Jess had permission to miss this class due to work and her standing in the culinary department, so Aurora had joined John and Calvin's group. Her tan, lightly freckled skin seemed magically and immediately to attract the flour. John spent several minutes wiping it from her eyes, cheeks, and forehead. Of course, the three of them found the whole event hilarious. If his dark looks thrown their way were any indication, Marcus did not appear to find it funny in the least. She shrugged his bad mood off. Someone must have hacked his computer she thought. This man is nothing like the person I talk to each night.

The yeast breads were set aside to rise and the class turned to the tasks of quick breads. Chef had invited them to bring in a favorite recipe if they had one, and Aurora had brought two. The pantry was well stocked, so Chef was sure all the possible ingredients would be available. Rori let Calvin and John pick which one to make and they chose pumpkin bread.

"Reminds me of the holidays," John said. "Since I live in Hawaii, this weather is perfect Christmas weather." He and Calvin had also narrowed down their choices for their presentation. They had narrowed the choices to the Philippines or Japan, but were hoping Chef would let them do Hawaiian food instead. They had made the case that the food of the islands was indeed distinct enough from 'normal' American food, so Marcus agreed that he could rightly classify it as a separate world region.

Within an hour, the smells in the classroom did indeed invoke memories of the holidays. Aurora always wondered why Americans picked the most hectic time of the year to add to their chores baking which was so labor intensive. She knew it was the sense of family that shared meals and shared treats brought. She missed her family and could hardly wait until next weekend. Her parents and sister were coming in on Saturday morning for the art show that evening and graduation on Sunday afternoon.

She was doubly excited to see her sister, who had just finished her senior year at the state university in their hometown. Gwen was a history major and they had tickets for a three-week European trip, leaving just a little less than a month after graduation. The trip was part of the reason Rori was so excited about this class. Before she had been planning to haunt the historically important art sites and spend hours in museums. Now, she felt a little more knowledgeable about the local cuisines.

The rest of class was uneventful, for once.

"I think it's really you that bugs Chef Charming," Rori teased Jess later that night. "With you not there, he completely ignored me today. I must have finally done something right." She did not realize how disappointed she sounded.

"You know my thoughts on the matter, girlie," Jess reminded her. She had told Rori that she thought Chef Marcus acted that way because he was secretly attracted to her. Rori had found the idea almost as ludicrous as Pastor Sam's suggestion that she was attracted to Marcus. Rori let Jess know she found her hypothesis hilarious and told her roommate so in no uncertain words.

"Methinks the girl doth protest too much," Jess laughed.

"Whatever," Rori rolled her eyes and tossed a pillow at her roommate, sounding more like a teenager than the mature young woman in her mid-twenties that she was.

She headed back to the studio after lunch and immersed herself in her paintings. She did not remember to break for dinner until almost nine o'clock when her stomach growled in protest.

The only other student in the studio called out, "Wow, Rori, do you have a lion in your cabinet or are you just that hungry?"

"Lion," she quipped back. "But he's hungry so I'm going to run out for a burger, do you want one?"

"No, I'm good," the senior art student replied, as she was cleaning up her paintbrushes. "I'm done for the evening. You promise you'll call security to follow you home if you stay much later, right?"

"Will do!" Rori said as she grabbed her wallet and headed for the exit. The night sky was clear and beautiful. Wishing she could just stretch out on the ground and drink in the beauty, Rori paused. Her stomach growled again and she laughed to herself. *It would be my luck anyway that if I did, Chef Charming would probably choose that very moment to walk out the door.*

The object of her ponderings was in fact watching her from his office window as she returned with her dinner. Marcus was working late in his office on the very idea he had brought up to Dr. Smith and was preparing a handout for the students.

She's out much too late for my comfort, he thought. *The art department needs to have better security if these young ladies are coming and going from the building at all hours of the night.*

He pulled out the class roster and grabbed his phone to text her. Hesitating, he decided on the safer, and less personal, route. His computer was already on, so he switched to his email account and pulled up her email address. It was first on his list, of course. It took several attempts to decide on the best wording. 'Dear Aurora,' versus 'Dear Ms. Sinclair," versus, "Ms. Sinclair,' was the biggest battle, but he eventually composed his admonishment.

Dear Aurora: I saw you leave the studio late this evening. I can't help but be concerned for the safety of the art students at such late hours. I must insist that you take better precautions. ~Marcus

Rori didn't get his message until much, much later. As she typed her response very early the next morning, she laughed at how appalled he would be had he known how late she really stayed. She had forgotten that he would see the time stamp on her email when he read it in the morning.

Already not happy with Rori when he saw the time of her response, her message really infuriated him.

Dear Lord (or is it Laird?) Marcus: (He still reminded her of a Scottish Highland lord, and she thought Officer Marcus too formal)

It will please you to know that I arrived at my dorm safe and sound, as I do every time I stay late at the studio. Please be assured I am old enough to not need parental supervision. Despite how I may act in your eyes, I am in fact an adult. ~ Delinquent Sinclair

P.S. Campus Security follows me home.

She added a smiley face, hoping childishly that it would irritate Marcus.

'Lord Marcus'? He was furious. Her tone was that of a two-year-old. That's it. I'm done. It will serve her right if she gets kidnapped by some lunatic one evening. As he walked into the church building, Marcus knew his thoughts were not conducive for a worshipful Sunday morning service, but he had promised Jake that he would meet him for the nine o'clock morning service.

Sporting a fresh Superhero bandage on her damaged finger, Rori gathered her children's Bible study lesson and headed to church. Jess was waiting patiently by her car.

"I'm coming, I'm coming," Rori called. "I didn't realize what a pain this finger would still be after two days," she explained her tardiness. "Even though I'm left-handed, there's a lot I never realized I used my right hand for!"

"Did you send Chef MacRae another message this morning?" Jess had heard her last night and felt free to pose her question as they drove the short distance to church. Normally they would walk, but the weather had decided to turn unseasonably warm. Plus, it would save Rori time getting back into the studio this afternoon.

"I know you thought your latest contribution to the literary field running between you two was hilarious," she said when Rori revealed the content of her original response to his email. "I can assure you there is a good possibility he will not find it funny at all."

A couple days earlier, Jess had caught Rori replying to one of Chef's emails and demanded all the details, as well as the right to see any future correspondence.

Rori had been reluctant when her roommate quite pointedly asked, "What are you trying to hide?" She felt obligated and strangely comforted by the accountability. Rori knew that her sense of humor and quirky view of life did not always translate well into other people's language. Especially tall, handsome Scottish ones.

"I apologized right before we left," Rori assured her. "He probably won't get it until after church." Of course, what she didn't tell Jessica was that her curt email simply said, *'Sorry,'* in response to the childish one she had sent earlier. No telling how he'll take that one, either, Rori thought.

Sitting on the opposite side of the sanctuary, Rori was unaware that Marcus had come to church with the Hamptons. He, on the other hand, had been diligently watching the doorway for her arrival. Now that he knew she was safely as far away from him as possible, he was relieved. At least he told himself he was relieved, but he didn't remember relief ever feeling like desolation before.

As the song portion of worship ended, the pastor dismissed the children for their separate Bible study time. Rori made her way across the front of the church gathering a following of four and five-years-olds like a pied piper. As the pastor announced a time of greeting for the adults, Rori and her entourage headed down an aisle just as Marcus stepped into it. He had moved aside to allow Zoe to join the throng. Turning to rein in one of the excited youngsters, Rori accidently plowed into Marcus.

"Oh, I'm so sorry," she said to the unknown person she had bumped into. "I was trying to keep Jimmy from running and wasn't watching where I was going." When saw that it was Marcus, she quickly bent down to pick up her craft and lesson plans that had dropped in the process.

His familiar hand reached down and pulled her to her feet. Marcus then bent and scooped up her supplies and handed them to her quickly. As he did, he saw her brightly colored bandage and froze. It seemed to mock him and his treatment of her and reminded him of the dismissive email he read this morning—an email he knew had been sent at two in the morning.

He retreated once again behind the curtain of aloofness that had become his only defense around this bewitching creature.

"Your bounty, Princess," he said, his tone cold, aloof, and slightly sarcastic.

He was mocking her! At church!

"Thank you, Chef," she bowed, adding a cynical *'Charming'* under her breath.

One last try, he promised himself. Hoping for an immediate response he chose to text her right after church.

I hope you made it to your children's class without any further mishaps. I apologize for my part in the catastrophe. I couldn't help but notice the bandage on your finger. Is it healing well?

Confusion ruled her thoughts. She was sure she hadn't mistaken his tone of voice when he helped her to her feet.

Well, if he wants to play make believe, I'll join right in. She thought.

Yes, thank you. I apologize for plowing into you.

He smiled at her quick response, and offered his immediately.

I also noted the unusual choice of superhero bandage. Why the famous green guy?

Ah, yes, the green guy. It may surprise you, Chef MacRae, to know that he and I are strangely similar creatures. Great bursts of emotion turn us into other-worldly beings. That's why people avoid making him angry.

And you? Marcus replied, wanting to continue the interchange.

Yes, I avoid making him angry too. I've got to go now. Thank you again for checking on me.

Jake's words, "She has a wicked sense of humor," immediately came to mind. I'm in way over my head, Marcus thought. But I'm enjoying every minute of it.

9
My Kingdom for a Croissant

By Monday, panic was setting in for Rori. She had completed all her major paintings Sunday evening. Normally she resisted working on Sundays, but the cooking class had cut into time she would have spent in the studio. *Why did I ever think that three-hour break each evening was going to be worth it?*

Although the paintings were complete, she had framing, descriptions, and printmaking preparations to do for the ones that would be available for sale. Thankfully, the school's art department was one of the best facilities in the state and had the equipment to scan her pieces, even the oversized ones, in order to make prints in the future. Those paintings that she didn't scan could be priced as one-of-a- kind originals. There were six of her twenty works like that, although she wasn't confident in their selling. She had watched the other four artists that were participating and their work was so different from her abstract nature pieces that she wasn't confident in hers.

Jessica, John, and Calvin all showed up at the studio to make sure she was coming. They waited patiently for her to change out of her overalls and into the same peasant skirt she had worn on the first day of class, this time matched with a peach t-shirt with one of her favorite art sayings: *Art is Man's nature. Nature is God's art. ~James Bailey.*

They were running down the hallway, the trio tugging Rori along just as Marcus stepped out to check on the racket. They all skidded to a stop and sheepishly made their way into class. How does he manage to make me feel like a child? He needs to loosen up! Her thoughts were a mixture of guilt and stubbornness.

As they entered the room through the door Marcus held open, she remembered that they were doing pastries tonight.

"Oh, this was the night I was most looking forward to!" she excitedly exclaimed.

"Glad I could be of service," Marcus's deep voice resounded in her ear. She jumped. She hadn't realized he was right behind her. He watched in fascination as her lightly tanned face colored with embarrassment. They stared at each other until she finally looked away. Score one for Chef Charming, she thought as she moved to join Jessica.

"Tonight, class, we will be learning about pastries." The chef turned his attention to the rest of his class. Unable to resist a dig, he added, "And I have it on very good authority that there are some of you who were greatly looking forward to this particular topic."

Rori groaned, but quietly enough that only Jess heard. Of course, her faithful roommate thought his comment was extremely humorous.

Class began with a boring basic vocabulary lesson, Jessica making notes in the margins of the handout Chef had provided as Rori just doodled on hers.

"Finally," she breathed to her roommate as the chef called them to the demonstration table. "I'm starving. I didn't get dinner."

"Again?" Jess chided her quietly. "You're going to get sick before your show if you don't take better care of yourself."

"I'll be fine," Rori said, "If he'd hurry up and make me some dinner!" The two friends laughed at her mockingly demanding tone.

Of course, their laughter aroused a raised eyebrow from Chef. How does he do that? Rori thought, watching the scornful brow arch over his eye. Amazing. She grinned mischievously at him.

"We'll start with croissants this evening," Chef continued. "These take several steps with overnight chilling time in-between. I started several batches earlier today, so you'll be able to observe each one. You will all have a chance to roll out the dough so you can get a feel for the process." The class divided into three groups and proceeded to follow the easy instructions. The pastries were not difficult to make, just time-consuming.

Jessica and Rori joined forces with the older couple and two young moms from the community. It was a delightful evening. After the croissants, Chef demonstrated several other techniques and the groups each chose a different delicious pastry to attempt.

As the nine o'clock hour approached, Marcus pulled out the coffee urn and the room filled with the smell of freshly brewing delightfulness. Rori was bordering on lightheadedness, due to skipping dinner and only eating a package of crackers for lunch.

"Sit down, young lady," Mr. Watkins, the elderly gentleman in their group insisted, as he saw her wobble slightly.

"I'm sorry," she confessed. "I forgot to eat since breakfast and I think I'm a little woozy."

Chef Marcus noticed the slight commotion and came over to the group that he had successfully avoided up until now. "Anything I can help with, Mr. Watkins?" Chef asked.

He's so nice to everyone else, Rori thought when she heard his kind tone.

"This young lady just needs to eat something, Chef," the grandfather answered, as his wife was handing Rori a wet towel. "She says she hasn't eaten since breakfast."

"Is this true Miss Sinclair?" Chef turned to his emotional nemesis.

"Yes, but I'll be okay as soon as our delicious cream puffs come out of the oven," she waved a hand towards their oven and covered her distress with quick words. "Should be any second now!" Go away, please, she wanted to add.

Seemingly ignoring her, Marcus marched to another group's table and snatched one of their already plated masterpieces, returned and pushed it at her.

"Eat. Now." Marcus commanded. Rori obeyed, wanting to mimic his tone with 'Me Tarzan, You Jane.' She knew she was in bad shape when her giddiness reverted to such childish humor.

She obediently stuffed the macaroon in her mouth, smiling around the delicious mouthful. "There," she said, "I'm good."

"Stay put until you are steady on your feet," Marcus insisted. "I don't want to have to rescue a fainting princess tonight."

Rori and Marcus didn't see the sly smiles exchanged between the Watkins, the young moms, and Jessica. Almost everyone in the class was aware of the undercurrents going on between the graduate art student and the handsome young chef. It had become quite the topic of conversation before and after class.

"It is quite obvious that neither of the interested parties knows the other is interested," Mr. Watkins commented.

That the rest of the class suspected what she did was news to Jessica.

"I promise all of you that I'll tell them both to wake up as soon as the course is over," she assured the group, out of Rori's earshot. "I think Chef MacRae thinks that the school has some regulation he would be violating if he showed any interest in a student. But she's a graduate student which makes her fair game, so to speak."

"I think he's just in denial because she's so different from him," the wise Mrs. Watkins spoke up. "It's like a breath of fresh air that he's not used to. They are perfect for each other." The romantic at heart smiled as the rest of the group agreed.

The coffee and pastries filled her growling lion of a stomach and Rori left class fully sated. She only returned to the studio to retrieve her backpack and wallet. She was heading straight home under orders from her pseudo doctors John and Calvin.

"Whatever is down there can wait," they insisted as Jess joined them to head out to late night bowling. "Go home!"

The light sprinkles from earlier in the day had turned into a full-fledged downpour as she ran across the sidewalk and jumped into her VW Beetle. This will be a fun ride home, she thought. Her windshield wipers were due to be replaced, but it was something she didn't think about until she needed them. Like tonight.

She was rubbing off the condensation from the car's poor ventilation when Marcus came out of the building. She saw that he had no umbrella as he began to walk down the block. She honked her horn, leaned over, and rolled down her window.

"Do you need a ride?" she asked. The rain would begin in earnest any minute now if the typical pattern held.

"No, I'll be fine." He was startled at the voice coming from the bright orange Volkswagen. An early seventies model, from what he could tell.

"Get in, you big stubborn oaf!" Rori demanded. For some strange reason, he obeyed.

As he folded himself into the tiny front seat, he wiped the rain from his face. She was obviously rain-soaked, too, but not as bad as he was.

"What did you call me?" Marcus turned to her, still not believing he had gotten into her car.

"A stubborn oaf." She thought he laughed, but she wasn't sure.

His apartment was only a couple of blocks away. Thankfully the rain let up slightly just as she pulled up to his building. Still Marcus hesitated before getting out of the car. Rori had no idea that he was grasping for an excuse to extend his stay. After what seemed like hours to him, but was in fact only a second, he remembered overhearing a conversation at her station tonight.

"Tell me the cream puff story," he said. "I heard the laughter but your little incident distracted me so I forgot to ask before class ended."

Rori smiled at the memory of her dad's culinary misadventure but was somewhat confused by the chef's attention.

"Are you sure?" she asked. "It's just a silly story about my dad."

"Yes, please," Marcus said. Hopefully the desperation wasn't evident in his voice.

Rori recounted the story. It happened during her home church's annual Dad's Dessert Contest. Professor Sinclair had won the previous year with an orange cake and was expanding his culinary skills with the more difficult cream puffs. Unfortunately, his wife and daughters were out shopping when he began his production. Not realizing that you should measure flour quite differently from brown sugar, he carefully packed down each of the four cups of all-purpose flour. As the cream puffs baked, they looked marvelous. As he pulled them out of their molds to cool, he realized something had gone terribly wrong. They were as heavy as baseballs. In fact, when his neighbor, a fellow dessert challenge competitor, came to the door later that afternoon, Dr. Sinclair tossed him one of the perfect looking creampuffs. Thankfully, the neighbor ducked, otherwise the cream puff would have knocked him out. After a lot of laughter and teasing, Rori's dad made another batch, which won him a second-place ribbon.

"So, your dad likes to cook?" Marcus asked.

"We call his cooking, 'creative'," Rori said. "He made a delicious homemade soup one time, mainly by combining various vegetables and spices. It was fantastic. Unfortunately, he had just grabbed random things from the cabinet and hadn't bothered to write anything down. There was no hope of duplicating it."

"He sounds a lot like my brother James," Marcus said. "I would love to meet him." Realizing too late to stop the words that conveyed more of his feelings than he was ready to acknowledge, he quickly opened the door of the car.

"See you tomorrow night," he said as he leaned in the open door. With no hint of command, but a sense of concern, he added, "Please try to eat before you come to class. Thanks for the ride, and for the story."

Who are you and what have you done with my disagreeable, mean chef? She wanted to ask. She stared in wonder.

"You're welcome," she said as he hauled himself out of her small car.

He seemed to hesitate, almost as if he wanted to say something more. Instead, he only added, "Goodnight, Aurora."

"Goodnight, Marcus," she said as he closed the car door.

When she got back to her apartment, she turned on her computer immediately to finalize her descriptions for the art show. Before she could begin, she heard her text notification from across the room. She purposely kept her phone out of reach so she could concentrate. She gave into the temptation and checked the message. It was from Marcus.

Thanks for the ride. Your carriage was exactly what I pictured yours would be. But it looks a little like a pumpkin. Aren't their rules against borrowing from other fairy tales?

Rori smiled. His sense of humor was peeking out again.

I was glad to be of service. I'd hate to think of you lying in a puddle in front of the Tech Building. Being made of sugar and all, I'm sure you were likely to melt.

His response wasn't immediate, and she started to return to her computer only to hear the text come through as she sat down. What she didn't know was that his fingers had hesitated over the keyboard. He decided to venture out on the proverbial limb, figuring it was much easier to do now, not in person.

You're very funny...I like the saying on your shirt. It reminds me of one of my favorite quotes about cooking. It's from Voltaire. 'Nothing would be more tiresome than eating and drinking if God had not made them a pleasure as well as a necessity.' Goodnight, Aurora.

He had also turned off his phone as soon as he sent the message, not brave enough to wait for her reply.

10
Soufflé Can You See?

Sorely tempted to skip tonight's class, Rori attended under protest. She was tired from her studio work, which now consisted mainly of packing up her supplies and preparing her work for transport on Thursday to the gallery.

The artist refused to admit to herself that the emotional war waging between her and Marcus was also taking a toll on her. Jessica had dropped broader and broader hints that their battles were just romantic tension. To combat this absurd notion, Rori added an expose on the thirteenth chapter of first Corinthians, commonly called the Love Chapter, to her sketch of Marcus at the back of her sketchbook. She had drawn a quick picture of him after the first class with a countdown of the twelve days of class. She marked off a day every morning. The title of the masterpiece was *You Shall Endure*.

Below the caricature she had scribbled, 'You can do anything for two weeks!' She quickly wrote out the passage, adding commentary:

"Love is patient...*Grumpy, annoyed, irritated*...Love is kind... *merciless, harsh*...

Does not envy, does not boast, is not proud.... (She paused and circled the note next to that entry)...*Need more info/background – ask Jake & Carla?*

She continued.

Does not dishonor others...not self-seeking.... *Seems to be ok here*...Not easily angered?!?... *Try infuriating... on edge*...keeps no records of wrongs...*Or has a photographic memory of every mistake I've made*....

Does not delight in evil but rejoices in truth.... *trust Jake's opinion, I guess?*...

Protects.... *Ok I'll give him that one*... (She drew a heart next to this one)

Trusts?... hopes*?*.... *expects the worst*...Always perseveres.... *Or is he counting down the days of torture like I am...?*

Thankfully, her sketchbook was rarely out of her sight so there was no danger in her mischief—or her feelings—being discovered.

Sitting in class waiting for Jessica to arrive, Rori flipped open the sketchbook. It was an addiction. She rarely was without a pencil or pen in hand, sketching on whatever surface she could find. Her notes in all her classes and even in sermons were covered with artwork.

She was the only one in the class. Even Marcus was nowhere to be seen. When she saw how early she was, she considered hanging around outside, but instead decided to be brave...here alone in the lion's den. She swallowed a giggle. Maybe he'll talk to me like we do online if I'm the only one here, she thought. Knowing that was probably a hopeless dream, and unwilling to think too much about why it was so important to her, she pushed the thoughts away.

She sketched fruit, vegetables, and loaves of bread and within minutes had covered a couple of pages with abstract, interesting drawings.

"Nice work," the deep voice behind her startled her. She jumped and dropped her pencil.

"Marcus," his name came unbidden. "You startled me."

His breath caught as her blue eyes met his, an involuntary smile on her lips. Marcus had seen her engrossed in her sketching and realized she had not heard his approach. Drawn to her like the cliché moth to a flame, he decided to delay the class preparations to steal a few moments alone with Miss Aurora Sinclair.

"Chef Marcus, in class please, Princess," he smiled as he handed her the dropped pencil. His fingers brushed the palm of her hand. The effect of his touch combined with the smile had a devastating effect on her breathing. She seemed to have forgotten how.

"Sorry," Rori bowed her head to recover her involuntary functions, such as breathing and heart beating, and to hide the blush she was sure was spreading across her face.

"These are quite good," Marcus was now thumbing through the five or six pages of food related items. "I knew you did portraits, but had no idea you had such an expansive repertoire. I'd be interested in using these for a project that Jake and I are working on." He smiled again.

I'm going to die right here at his feet, Rori thought. *I can see the headlines now: 'Coed falls victim to handsome chef's deadly smile'.* She laughed.

"What's so funny about that?" Marcus asked, his smile fading. Is she laughing at me, again? He thought disappointedly.

"No, no," Rori tried to recover. "I'm just not used to you being nice to me. Sorry." Avoiding eye contact, she did not see the devastating affect her words had on Marcus.

"That would be great," she continued, unaware of his painful confusion. "You're welcome to use whatever sketches you need. Would you like me to drop some by to you or Jake before Friday?"

Marcus struggled to regain his equilibrium. Apparently, her comment had not been meant to wound since she blithely continued their previous conversation.

"Maybe you could meet with me and Jake about it one morning?" He suggested. Last night he finally admitted that since his time with this frustrating and fascinating woman was coming to an end, he needed to act soon. He was desperate and terrified all at the same time.

"Say, Friday morning?" He asked.

"Okay," Rori agreed hesitantly. "You do remember that I won't be in class Friday night, right?"

Why do you think I want to see you on Friday morning? Chef thought. Knowing that would shock her for sure, he decided against verbalizing his thoughts.

"Yes, I remember," he replied instead. "You have a preview for your art show, correct?"

"Yes." She nodded anxious to end this uncomfortable intimacy as the other students were entering the lab. "I can meet you and Jake at the cafeteria Friday, say around eight thirty? Is that okay?"

"See you then." He closed her sketchbook and moved away.

Rori could breathe again. Now if only her heart would behave, she might actually survive the evening.

The soufflés were tricky but fun, and messy, so Rori thoroughly enjoyed them. Jessica said that Rori never used the same spoon, or pot, or pan, or potholder, if she could take one, or two, or all the others out of the drawers, instead. Their station was a wreck, but their broccoli and cheese soufflé was delicious.

"This is definitely a skill I will practice," Rori said. "I'm going to make my parents a fancy breakfast before Gwen and I go to Europe."

"You really ought to ask him tonight, you know," Jess reminded Rori about their weekend discussion. Jessica had suggested that she ask Marcus to make some culinary recommendations for her upcoming European adventure.

"You know, like what foods to try in Paris, and the best pastry shop in Rome, things like that." Jess was trying everything she could to push these two lovebirds together. "I'm sure he would love to give you some ideas."

Rori reluctantly agreed to speak to him after class. Their planned meeting on Friday morning made for a perfect excuse. She made Jessica promise to stay with her while she talked to him.

"Just in case he says something to make me mad. I wouldn't want to hurt him without a witness," Rori giggled.

"Chef MacRae," her roommate stopped him before he headed to his office. "We have a special request." Jess decided not to give Rori a chance to change her mind.

"How can I be of service, ladies?" Marcus had been frantically thinking of excuses to engage in another conversation with Aurora. It was like an answer to prayer.

Jess launched right in, "Rori and her sister are going to Europe and she needs some input on places, and food, you would recommend she try."

"My sister is graduating with a degree in History next week," Rori explained as the handsome man smiled, turning his full attention to her. "It's our dual graduation gift from our parents and grandparents." Stop doing that, she thought, fascinated as the smile transformed his demeanor. It's not fair!

"How nice," Marcus pulled up a stool and pulled out a notebook. "Tell me exactly where you're going and I'll work on some ideas. Will Friday morning at breakfast be soon enough?"

Jessica was not aware of their previous engagement and raised startled eyebrows.

"Yes, that would be fine," Rori ignored her roommate. "We're going to London, Paris, Rome, and Florence. The travel agent also arranged some open days for us with flexible arrangements so we can make some detours, too. We'll end up back in England, where we want to take the last few days touring the countryside and," she hesitated, "Scotland."

"Ah, the motherland," Marcus broke into a thick Scottish accent. "I've been to visit twice and a lovely land it is indeed."

Jessica's giggles were infectious. Rori was beet red, but couldn't help but laugh, too.

"It's hopeless isn't it?" Rori asked her roommate as they walked away from the building, the cool crisp air a welcome relief on her still blushing face. "Does he have any idea how adorable he is?"

Adorable was not a common word used to describe the six-foot-tall red headed chef, Jessica thought.

"You've got it bad, sweetheart. What happened to the repugnant, stubborn, impatient, mean, unreasonable man you met last week? He doesn't seem any different to me," Jess teased Rori.

"Be quiet," Rori pretended to pout. "It's just a silly infatuation. Plus, I'm leaving town next Tuesday morning and will likely never see him again." Why did the thought depress her so much?

11
Sweet Desserts, Don't Desert Me

Wednesday morning Rori and Jessica worked on their project. Chef was letting them do their presentation on Thursday since Rori would be missing Friday's class. They had indeed settled on Italian food and were doing four dishes: two in the northern style and two in the more traditional southern style. Rori was in charge of the report and shopping for the ingredients. She also wanted to be solely in charge of one dish, so she chose Savoiardi, known to most Americans as ladyfingers. Baking had been her favorite part of the class so far, and she didn't feel she could conquer the more difficult tiramisu, which used ladyfingers soaked in espresso. Jess was doing a polenta dish, preferred by many to pasta in the north, and they were working together on a traditional pizza from the southern region and a fish soup, popular at Christmastime.

The report and presentation were easy to accomplish and Jess made a detailed list of ingredients for Rori. Volunteering to do the shopping was another way to keep her mind off the studio, art show, and Chef Marcus. Jessica was not fooled one bit. Shopping meant she didn't have to be the one to meet with the chef to go over their dishes.

"Finally. Desserts!" John and Calvin exclaimed as they rushed into Wednesday's class, running late due to packing up their dorm apartment. Calvin was a Residence Hall Director and John was his roommate. Calvin was getting married later in the summer and his wife, Sally, would be moving in.

"The place should smell much better next year," Calvin had deadpanned during one of their after-class coffee trips last week.

"Okay, class," Marcus called for their attention. "Tonight is our last night of cooking. We're going out with everyone's favorites. Desserts." There were cheers and groans of delights. The lab already smelled heavenly, since Marcus had begun some dishes earlier in the day.

"At your stations you will find three recipes. Choose one to prepare," he continued. "For those taking this class for credit, this will count as a test grade, so I will not be assisting you as much as I normally do. You should all have mastered the skills required."

He saw looks of panic from several of the less confident students, including Aurora. Seeking to encourage her, he added, "I promise. It will be very, very easy. I know you all will be shocked to know, I'm not really a mean guy."

Why is he looking at me? Rori thought. Am I that obvious?

The Watkins, Jess and the boys, and even the two moms exchanged knowing looks. "Oh yes, dear," the matron whispered to her husband, "You're definitely correct. They are head over heels."

Chef made his way around the classroom during the course of the evening. He stopped at Jessica and Rori's station and swiped a finger full of their cheesecake filling,

"Delicious," he said licking his lips. "Good job. Any problems with the spring pan?"

"No," Jessica answered for Rori as she watched her roommate be mesmerized at the chef's simple gesture. I wonder if Rori realizes she's staring at his lips, she thought.

As the classmates sat around the classroom later enjoying the fruits of their labor, Marcus watched the group of four that usually drew his attention. John was wiping whipped cream from Rori's nose and she was playfully patting his cheek with her powdered sugar covered hand. His previously light mood darkened. He wanted to do the young man bodily harm.

As class was wrapping up, Marcus reminded the four groups that were presenting tomorrow night to check with him before they left. This was Jess's job since Rori was doing the shopping.

"I'll see you eight here bright and early to get your dishes started. One of each group needs to come see me before you leave to make sure everything will be ready for you." He was relieved to see Jess walking towards him and not Aurora. Coward, he said to himself. Luckily for John, Calvin was the spokesman for their group.

Later that night, unable to resist what had become an addiction, Marcus opened his email program and typed. He logged into his personal account to skirt the danger presented by to use the class account to continue personal correspondence not related directly to the class.

Dear Aurora: I know you are busy with your art show. Are you nervous about your presentation? Do you or Ms. Johnston have everything you need? Let me know if there's anything I can do to help. ~Marcus

Aurora had just logged on to check for a message from her parents. They were making final plans for the weekend and she wanted to double-check their arrival time. They were also sending her links for her Europe trip. Clicking on the message box, she responded to Marcus first out of habit.

Dear Marcus: I think we're good. I'm doing the shopping early in the morning and then meeting Jessica at nine. Class was delicious tonight. ~Aurora.

Dear Aurora: Well, you and John Liu seemed to certainly be enjoying it. ~Marcus

Wondering if his jealousy was evident or if he should change the font color to green, he hesitated, but sent the message anyway.

Rori was slightly confused. He almost sounded jealous, but she convinced herself that they must have just gotten a little too loud for Chef's liking.

Marcus: Sorry to be disruptive...again! John is so besotted with Jessica it's hilarious. I've threatened him on numerous occasions. If he doesn't ask her out by

Saturday, I'm going to bop him on the head. Apparently, he did not take my powdered sugar threats tonight seriously, since she is still moping around here hoping for a phone call. Why are guys so dense? ~Aurora

Relief that washed over Marcus. He wanted to reach through the computer and kiss this young woman until she giggled for release. She thinks John has it bad. If she only knew.

Aurora: I apologize on behalf of all us men-types. I agree. We are dense and clueless most of the time when it comes to understanding women. You should all feel sorry for us. ~Marcus.

Oh, I do! Aurora replied, pausing to insert an image of a silly face to her message. *I have to go. My dad is calling. See you tomorrow. ~Aurora.*

Goodnight, Aurora. ~Marcus

12
To Europe or Not to Europe?

Thursday's gloomy rain-swept morning matched Rori's mood. The call from her dad had brought bittersweet news. Gwen had received a prestigious job offer to teach at a new school in their district. She was thrilled, but it meant cancelling their European trip. There was no one to take Gwen's place on such short notice.

Thankfully, they had purchased trip insurance from the travel agent so most of the money would be refunded. Her dad had encouraged her to wait at least a week before officially cancelling her trip. They would try to find someone else to go with her, and besides they had until forty-eight hours before the first flight to cancel.

Shopping for the ingredients was a breeze since Jess had provided a detailed list. Even the sights and smells of the market did not cheer Rori.

Marcus was so attuned to her by now that he immediately knew something was wrong when she walked through the door. He pulled Jessica aside.

"Is everything okay?" he asked. At this point, he did not care if Miss Johnston thought his inquiry was unusual. He did not know that she knew about his and Rori's late night conversations.

"Yes, it will be fine," Jessica said, only partially surprised at his concern. "Rori just got a bit of bad news last night."

"Nothing serious, I hope," Marcus continued. "Mom and Dad are okay, right?"

"Yes, just a bit of a disappointment, nothing earth-shattering." Jess said, trying not to smile at his barely disguised interest.

"Okay." Marcus moved away, not completely reassured by Jessica's words. He was extremely curious about what was troubling Aurora, but resisted the urge to push the issue further. "I'll be in my office if there's anything anyone needs. I'm sure you'll be able to handle any emergencies, Miss Johnston."

The groups worked on the dishes steadily and the aromas filled the classroom. Rori was very quiet. The two weeks were taking their toll. Her art display was almost complete. She had stopped by the studio on her way back from the grocery store to check on her last oil painting. It needed to be dry so she could move it and her last two large pieces to the gallery in the morning. After breakfast with Marcus and Jake.

"Oh, I forgot about breakfast," Rori groaned. Jess looked at her in concern. She just shook her head quickly, adding, "It's nothing, I'm okay." The roommate wisely let the matter drop.

The presentations that evening went well. Even she and Jess did well, despite her distraction and disappointment. Rori had heard again from her father and he reiterated his suggestion that she not panic.

He reminded her in his calm, professor voice, "God is in control, even of silly young girls who panic over silly European trips and silly logistical problems." Her dad cracked her up sometimes with his lame attempts at humor. Still, it had served her well. She admitted that considering world events, and the universe, not being able to go to Europe in four weeks was a minor deal. Not that she was any happier about it, but she was in a calmer state tonight.

"Marvelous, class," Marcus saluted the four groups at the end of the evening. "We have had a wonderful world tour. Our trip tonight took us to lovely Italy," nodding to Jessica and Rori, "through Asia and the Pacific islands, "indicating the two young moms who had chosen Chinese food, and John and Calvin's Hawaiian fare, "and my personal favorite, hearty food from the United Kingdom. Thank you all. I look forward to tomorrow night." Several people in class that had noted Chef's use of the word 'lovely' in reference to Jessica and Rori's presentation.

As they cleaned up and shuffled out of the room, he reminded them to pick up the study guide for their final exam, which would be on Saturday morning. "I promise it'll be the easiest exam you'll ever have."

"See you in the morning, Princess?" Marcus asked her as she picked up the two-page handout.

"Yes, Chef," Rori answered. She was so exhausted that she didn't see his desolate look as she seemed to brush off his inquiry. "Goodnight."

Hours later, Marcus paced his apartment. He decided that it was now or never. Jake was hounding him ruthlessly over taking a step forward before it was too late. "She's moving home on Tuesday, remember?"

Text or email...Marcus deliberated. Glancing at the clock, he saw it was close to midnight. Remembering how exhausted she seemed, he chose email, hoping not to wake her.

Dear Princess Aurora: I hope everything is okay. You seemed sad tonight. I will be praying for you. I look forward to breakfast tomorrow. Yours, Marcus.

He backspaced and changed 'Yours' to 'Sincerely' and back again before hitting send, doubtful she would even notice.

Rori had fallen into bed in an exhausted sleep immediately after class, and slept through her alarm, so left for breakfast without checking her email.

13
The Breakfast Calamity

A good night's sleep having gone a long way to restoring her optimism, Rori was already enjoying her second cup of coffee as Jake and Marcus joined her at the corner table she had chosen. They had laden their trays with an array of hearty breakfast foods.

"How can you eat that much in the morning?" she asked them, laughing as they jostled each other for table space. She held her sketchbook over her head in mock protection. "Watch out you two, or you'll ruin my masterpieces."

Finally clearing space by combining some of their side dishes onto a bigger plate, and stacking the extra empties on a neighboring table, they settled in.

"Are you not eating anything?" Marcus asked. "Didn't you learn your lesson earlier this week?"

Jake raised an eyebrow in response to his friend's pointed attention to Rori's eating habits, and smiled to himself. This was so much fun, he thought. About time, Mr. McLoner got his comeuppance.

"I'll go get some toast in a minute. Here are the sketches that you saw earlier, Marcus," Rori blushed slightly at using his name in front of his friend. She had long ceased referring to him by anything else in her mind.

As the two chefs tackled their feasts, she pointed out her favorites from the forty or fifty quick sketches she had done. They argued back and forth good-naturedly about their preferences, each insisting they had the better artistic eye.

"Art is a personal thing, gentlemen," Rori inserted into their mock disagreement. "Besides, we aren't talking about the Sistine Chapel here. It's just a student cookbook, right?"

"Speaking of the Sistine Chapel," Marcus reached for a folder in his backpack. "Here are my suggestions for your trip." He watched as her face fell. "What's wrong?"

"My sister was unexpectedly offered a job and won't be able to go. Looks like I'm going to have to postpone my adventure." The disappointed lady explained, "Jess doesn't have an up-to-date passport, and my mom can't take off that much time from work."

"Well, maybe you can find someone else to go with you," Jake said, nudging his best friend with his foot under the table. He received a shark kick in response. "Ouch!" he cried. "I mean, that's a bummer!"

"I'm going to go refill my coffee," Rori said as she rose from the table. "I could bring you both something to round out your meager meal," she offered dryly, eyeing their numerous empty plates. Before walking away, she turned back to Marcus. "And yes, Lord Marcus, I will get something to eat."

"Lord Marcus?" Jake asked after Rori made her way to the now long food line.

"Inside joke," Marcus mumbled, now thumbing through Rori's spiral bound sketchbook.

"Do you think you should be doing that without permission?" Jake asked, noticing that the food pictures were just a small portion of the work in the book.

Suddenly, Marcus froze. As he reached the end of the book, the image of his face on the last page seemed to mock him. It was an absurd caricature, complete with devil's horns and a lopsided halo.

"Marcus, I don't think this is a good idea," his friend's voice held a warning. "That is obviously not something she intended for you to see."

Marcus was beyond reason as he noticed a set of twelve boxes, entitled "Countdown to the End of My Misery" representing each of the ten classes. All but Friday and Saturday's boxes were checked off. The words 'You can do this' were written and underlined in the margin.

Below the timeline was the beautiful passage of scripture from Corinthians. Beside each line, the Princess had added commentary, pointedly directed at him and his character.

"Wow," he said as he read the first few lines. "I had no idea she hated me so much. She should have majored in theater where her tremendous acting skills would be put to better use."

He was furious. He grabbed a pen and checked off Friday and Saturday's boxes.

"And to think I thought I was falling in love with this woman." His words conveyed his fury and despair. "Princess? More like Prima Dona."

"Wait, Marcus," Jake tried to calm down his friend. "Don't do anything foolish. Give her a chance to explain."

As she returned to the table, Rori knew something was very wrong. Marcus had risen and was angrily stuffing the list for her trip into his backpack and zipping with furious motions. She glanced at the table and saw her sketchbook open to the picture of Marcus.

"Oh no!" Her words were barely audible as her knees buckled and she slumped into the chair Jake had pulled back out for her. Marcus stood fuming, his green eyes boring accusingly at hers, which were filling with tears.

"You weren't supposed to see that."

"Too late," Marcus stated. Too late for everything, he said to himself, bitter and disheartened. "You will notice that I have released you from the onerous duty of coming to class tomorrow morning," pointing to the check marks he had added. "I'll adjust your grade accordingly. You are officially exempt from the final exam. Good day, Miss Sinclair."

Jake stood and attempted to stop his friend.

"Don't be a fool, Marcus," he repeated his plea. "Let her explain."

"I'm done being a fool, Jake," Marcus spat out. "But, thanks for your concern."

As he stormed off, Rori wiped quiet tears. She did not want to admit to herself that the tears were from anything more than exhaustion.

"I'm sorry, Rori," Jake tried to comfort her. "He's a bit of an idiot sometime. I think he will come around. You just seem to push all his buttons." In more ways than you can imagine, Jake thought.

"I know he hates me," Rori said quietly, "but I thought we had begun a sort of friendship. The last few days were so much better. I was even going to invite him the art show." She refused to add the real motive behind her proposed invitation.

"Hate is definitely not what he feels for you," Jake muttered mysteriously. "Don't give up hope, okay?"

"Well, it's not my first experience with rejection," she said dejectedly. "I guess I was foolish to think this time would be any different."

Jake was slightly confused, but knew this was his opportunity to get to the truth from at least one of the two involved in this fiasco.

"What do you mean? Why do you think his reaction was rejection?"

She shrugged and ate her toast. It tasted like cardboard, but she didn't want to give Chef Charming any more fuel for his fire. The last thing she needed was to faint at the preview tonight and have word get back to him. She knew he would immediately assume she had purposely not eaten to spite him.

"It doesn't really matter now." Rori started to slip the offending sketchbook into her shoulder bag.

"Wait," Jake stopped her. "Can I see the picture again?"

"You can have it for all I care," she said morosely, tearing it out of her sketchbook and handing it to him. "I don't care to ever see it again." Jake set the picture aside and gave her a quick hug before she left.

"I'm praying for you two, also," he added.

"Thanks," Rori said, adding with a half-hearted grin, "I think." Jake laughed.

"I'll be okay, I promise, Jake. I'm just exhausted. If I can get through tonight, tomorrow night should be fun and then I get to graduate and get out of here!" Somehow, her unenthusiastic tone did not make her words believable.

After she left, Jake sat in stunned silence as he read her words at the bottom of the sketchbook page.

I am finally truly in love and yet 'Happily Ever After' seems just as far away as ever.

Jake realized that Marcus, in his typical hotheaded fashion, had not read past the first few lines on the page.

"I can't wait to tell Carla that she was right!"

Across campus, Rori collapsed on her bed in dejected despair. Jessica sat on the floor, begging her roommate to tell her what happened.

"I can't fix this unless you tell me what he said," Jess pleaded.

"This can't be fixed," Rori muttered. "The page made my feelings perfectly clear, and he just stormed out. Obviously, he has no interest in me at all. What you think you saw was completely wrong."

"Where is the sketch?" Jessica asked. She had seen the masterpiece and knew that it had been done in frustration. She also knew that Rori's last addition to it probably revealed more of her true feelings. Jess suspected Marcus had not read the whole page.

"I gave it to Jake. Hopefully he will burn it," Rori said. "Please, can we just drop this? I want to forget about the whole torrid mess. I wish I had never taken the class and never met Chef Marcus MacRae."

"You know that's the farthest thing from the truth," Jessica said as she prepared to go to work. "But I'll let you wallow in your sorrow. I have to go to work. Try to get some rest."

Minutes later, Jessica sat across from Jake in his office. She in fact didn't have to be at work for a couple of hours.

"What are we going to do about this?" she asked Chef MacRae's best friend. "I am so angry with Chef Charming I can hardly see straight."

"Chef Charming?" Jake laughed. "Is that what she calls him? That's priceless."

"Well, he teased her the first night over her name, calling her Princess Aurora," Jess answered Jake's questioning look. "You know, Sleeping Beauty."

"That's hilarious! I may have to use that one some time," Jake laughed. Turning the conversation back to their dilemma, Jake continued. "And as far as being furious with Marcus, join the club!"

"If he had taken the time to look at the whole page, her feelings would have become quite clear," Jess explained. "The whole reason she did the sketch in the first place was because she was battling her attraction for him from day one."

"I'm sure he didn't read more than the first couple of lines, if anything," Jake said. "I think he was mainly reacting to the picture and her countdown to the end of the class, treating it like a prison sentence she was enduring."

"Unfortunately, she thinks he read the whole thing and knows that she has feelings for him," Jess explained. "She thinks he's rejecting her."

"This is just getting worse and worse," Jake said. "I will tell you this, though. He's going to be devastated when he finds out how he blew it."

"Good," Jessica said. "Maybe that will get him to act before it's too late. Before this morning, I would have bet my last dollar that she was irrevocably and totally in love with him, but now she is so sure he wants nothing to do with her that it will take some major convincing skills to get her to accept the truth."

"He does love her, doesn't he?" Jessica thought she knew the answer, but asked anyway.

"Oh, yes," Jake said. "Definitely. But now, with this misinformation, I'm pretty sure he thinks it's hopeless."

They sat in silence, contemplating their next move.

"They're completely clueless, aren't they?" Jake laughed.

"Yes," Jess agreed. "How do we convince Chef Charming to woo Princess Aurora?"

"Well, for sure I'm going to drag him, kicking, and screaming if needed, to the art show. I think he'll admit that he owes her that much."

"She was hoping to have him meet her parents," Jess spilled Rori's secret. "I think I had finally gotten her to admit her feelings and at least give the guy a chance. I hope it's not too late."

"Well, I will get Carla and her Bible study group praying," Jake grinned. "Who better to call to arms than a group of young romantic newlywed ladies? They're all natural matchmakers. Not that I would mind having my best friend in the same state of happy captivity that I so nobly endure."

Jessica headed to work, calling Rori's mom before her shift started. She arranged to meet with her roommate's parents alone before the art show. She knew they needed to know about the unfolding romance.

By Friday afternoon, the last of her artwork was set up at the gallery, and her placards were in place. Rori stood back and admired her work.

She was still debating whether to submit the piece she had just finished. She didn't like the title, or the subject matter, for that matter. Of course, twelve hours ago it was the most treasured piece she had ever created. Now she didn't even want it on display. Professor Smith insisted. The piece, done in oil, was not very large. The tag held the all-significant letters "NFS" meaning it was "Not for Sale."

"Are you sure you want to let this one go, now?" Dr. Smith asked again. "At least put it up for the evening's silent auction with a higher reserve price." The professor knew there had to be a back-story to her change of heart.

"The auction is fine," Rori insisted. "But only put fifty dollars as my starting point. That will cover the cost of supplies. I don't need, or want, the piece anymore."

The preview turned out to be a relaxing evening for Rori. She had taken a long three-hour nap in the afternoon and soaked in a warm bath before the preview. Not having to face Marcus tonight was a huge relief. She was almost giddy with relief. It didn't hurt that the Preview was reserved for the movers and shakers of the University, as well as all the art department professors and their spouses. These people were some of her favorite and closest friends. She would miss them all but enjoyed the relief of the sophisticated cocktail party atmosphere of the evening.

14
Let the Show Begin

During Friday night's class Jess had been unable to keep her feelings hidden, she glowered at Marcus. He studiously avoided her gaze the rest of the evening. As she was leaving, though, he mentioned that because of her other culinary training, she did not necessarily have to take the "exam" tomorrow. He was planning to give the class an easy test to show them how much they had learned. He was hoping Miss Johnston would choose not to come because he wanted to avoid anyone involved in any way with Her Royal Princess, Aurora Sinclair.

"Like I'd miss the class party," Jessica commiserated with Rori late that night after the preview. "I still think you should thumb your nose at him and go anyway." Rori just shook her head slightly. Jess let the matter drop.

Jess left for the class party Saturday morning, sneaking out without waking Rori. Despite her worry over the situation, Jess enjoyed the affair. She should have skipped it, but she couldn't resist seeing how Marcus was holding up. Rori was a mess. Thankfully, her parents would be arriving later this morning.

Jess made a point of reminding John and Calvin about the art show within earshot of Chef Charming. Although Jessica knew Chef Hampton promised to get him to go no matter what, she decided it wouldn't hurt to have a little jealous competition. She had seen the jealous looks Marcus had leveled at the young man over the course of the class. What Marcus didn't know was that John had finally gathered enough courage to ask Jess out and the art show was to be their first official date.

"I know it would mean so much," Jess oozed, "especially for you to be there, John." If the glower on Marcus' face was any indication, he had taken the bait. John and Calvin were completely aware of what she was doing, since Jess had explained it all before class. The young men heartily agreed that their professor needed a bit of a reality check.

Jess couldn't resist, turning to the seething chef, "You should come, too, Chef MacRae. I'm sure Rori would be *thrilled* to see you," adding a wide smile for emphasis.

"Thank you for the invitation, Miss Johnston," Chef ground out through clinched teeth, "But I'm sure I have some other plans for tonight." He turned abruptly and stomped into his office, closing the door with a thud. It was obvious to Jess that Jake had not had a chance to clear things up with the stubborn man.

The trio barely held their laughter until they got outside.

Sitting with her parents at her favorite diner in town, Rori was able to relate the events of the past two weeks fairly objectively. Only a few tears were shed, but she had resolved to move on with her life. Obviously, this foolish fantasy she had dreamed up was just that – both foolish and fantasy.

Her parents were curious to meet the enigmatic man who had their eldest daughter in such a state. Without Rori's knowledge, Jessica had been able to fill in some of the details that Rori left out. Professor and Mrs. Sinclair and were now expectedly looking forward to the evening. It promised to be quite entertaining.

Across town, Marcus was also receiving some clarification and chastisement. He had received a call demanding his presence at the local pizzeria.

"What have I done?" Staring at the sketch, Marcus's shoulders slumped in misery. A long talk with Jake revealed what Jess had said about the sketch that had ruined his life.

"You really think we have a chance?" Marcus asked Jake. "I'm pretty sure I blew it completely yesterday. I can't imagine that she will ever forgive me."

"Well, you won't know if you don't try," Jake told him. Reluctantly, Marcus agreed to go to the show.

Leaving the restaurant, Marcus should have headed straight home, but instead found himself in front of Rori's dorm. Her silly car was still outside. He headed back home and called Jake.

"I know it's late to be changing my mind, but I don't think I can do it," frantic fear sounding in every word. "I'm not going to the show. I can't face her."

"You sound desperate, my friend," Jake tried to comfort his unsure friend.

"You, Carla, and Miss Johnston all seem to be so sure, but what if this is just something I've imagined?" His voice clearly showing the turmoil he was experiencing, he was miserable. "Tell me again that I'm not crazy to pursue this. I still do not believe in love at first sight, but this woman is in my blood and I don't think I'm going to get over this."

"We talked this over and over, Marcus. You need to step out on faith and trust that maybe, just maybe God is bringing you two together. And you heard the same advice from Pastor Collins, didn't you?" Jake reminded him of their conversation with the assistant pastor after church last Sunday. At the time, Marcus was frustrated with trying to avoid Rori and his growing feelings for her. What he didn't know was that Pastor Sam had watched in awe as the young culinary instructor talked about the very young lady that had stopped by to see him early in the week.

Indeed, God works in mysterious ways, Sam Collins had thought.

Bringing Marcus back to his present misery, Jake resorted to only half-joking threats.

"If you don't show up, I'll come find you and drag you there," he threatened. "I never expected such cowardly behavior from Chef Charming."

"Chef Charming?" Marcus asked curiously.

"Oops," Jake pretended the slip was unintentional. "That's what Rori calls you. I think it's kind of sweet, Princess Aurora and Chef Charming."

"Maybe I should ride into the gallery on a white horse," Marcus muttered, but Jake heard the beginnings of a slight smile.

"Marcus," Jake decided the time for joking was done, and straight talk was needed. "You love this woman and she loves you. God has brought you together. Don't waste this opportunity. End of discussion."

"Thank you, Jake," Marcus hung up the phone finally hopeful again.

Rori had to be at the art gallery an hour before the opening. Dressed in a green and blue evening gown with layers of different colors creating the scarf hem, she looked every bit an elf princess. The spaghetti straps exposed her honey-toned shoulders. The turquoise pendant on her gold chain added to her air of regality. Her long hair, loosely held by a hair clip, was adorned with a peacock feather that matched the tones of her gown.

Normally so casual about her outfits, even Rori had to admit she looked quite good tonight. It helped her feel confident, almost as though armed for battle. Thankfully, I won't have to slay any red-haired lions tonight. I'm sure Chef Charming Marcus MacRae is glad he's seen the last of me.

Her parents were among the first guests to arrive. They had met many of her professors on a previous visit to the campus, so they headed right in to look at their daughter's competition. Her dad promised to outrageously overpay for one of her 'silly scribbles,' as he jokingly called them. She knew he in fact was very proud and envious of her talent.

About an hour into the three-hour showing, she and her parents were discussing the silent auction. She explained that the pieces available were marked, pointing to the special tag on 'Aurora's Castle'. Bidders would head to the table at the back of the gallery and register their highest offer for the pieces they wanted. Their bids, sealed in individual envelopes, would be opened after the show ended later this evening. The winners would be contacted in the morning.

"Rori," came Jake's voice behind her, "I'd like to meet your parents. And tell them how you misbehave in Sunday School all the time." She and Jake were always battling each other with puns and silly comments during class. Carla was very tolerant.

Rori turned and felt the color drain from her face. Marcus was with Jake and Carla.

"What are *you* doing here?" Rori blurted.

"Aurora Grace Sinclair!" Dr. Donnie Sinclair said gently, but firmly. "That was quite rude. You should apologize to this nice young man."

"I apologize, Chef MacRae," Rori said, not quite sincerely. Marcus seemed to find her discomfort amusing.

"Marcus," he reminded her.

"I apologize, Chef Marcus," she knew she was baiting him, but couldn't help herself.

"Just Marcus." One eyebrow rose.

"I apologize, *Just Marcus*." She crossed her arms, unwilling to budge.

"You win," Marcus laughed, adding mysteriously, "for now." He turned to her father and introduced himself. Rori's father had watched their interplay with amused delight.

"Dr. Sinclair, Mrs. Sinclair, my name is Marcus MacRae. I've had the pleasure of Aurora's presence in my gourmet cooking class over the last two weeks." Her parents nodded and smiled, falling immediately under his spell.

Traitors, thought Rori.

"It's been interesting," Marcus added, turning back to her. "Miss Sinclair," Marcus held out his hand. "I look forward to seeing your art this evening. Could I beg a personal tour?" She is gorgeous, he thought.

She nearly choked. "Of course," was all she could manage.

Thankfully, Jake came to her rescue and made the rest of the introductions. He then asked Rori to show Carla the work of one of her classmates as soon as she was done with Marcus. These particular pieces were fascinating multi-media works that fooled the eye from a distance, only to reveal that they were indeed just household objects cleverly arranged.

Marcus pulled Rori's hand through his arm and nodded to her parents. "I look forward to visiting with you, if I could, as soon as Aurora shows me her works."

"It would be our pleasure," her mother said, smiling at the handsome young man. As she and her husband watched the couple walk away, they shared a knowing look.

"Oh my," Rori's mom said. Looks like we may be planning a wedding soon. This thought she kept to herself, knowing her husband would insist that she was rushing things.

As Rori led Marcus toward her paintings, the frustration over the sketchbook picture, and the realization that this was the end of her hopeful dreams of a life with this man, had lent Rori a dose of courage. She planned to hold nothing back.

"Chef, could you please explain something to me?" She turned to him as they moved out of earshot from their group.

"It's Marcus," he insisted again, "and certainly. Your wish is my command."

"Why can you call me whatever you want, 'Princess', 'Aurora', 'Your Highness', 'Miss Sinclair', 'Rori'," she began.

"I've never called you 'Rori'," he interrupted.

"You're right," she conceded, "but that's beside the point. Why do I have such restrictions on what I call you? And why do you keep switching what you call me? Does it show what mood you're in or is it all part of an act? When you think of me, not that you ever do, what name do you use in these musings?" Rori knew she was treading on dangerous ground but couldn't seem to help herself.

"You wouldn't believe me if I told you," Marcus said, smiling at the thought of her reaction to an honest answer. He knew his most common name for her over the last few hours was 'wife'. His smile widened into a grin.

"I'm glad you find me so amusing," Rori grumbled and let the topic drop. Remembering how mad he was as he stormed out of breakfast yesterday, she was baffled by his current behavior. She proceeded to show him her paintings, trying to sound objective and informative. He admired the paintings, genuinely impressed with her unique style, but spent a large part of the tour watching her animation as she explained her art. He wanted desperately to tell her what was in his heart, but had promised himself to speak to Dr. Sinclair first.

After they returned to her parents, Rori led Carla to the section of the gallery with her classmate's unusual works. They moved away from the group, Jake's wife asking questions about each piece as they moved through the gallery. Her instructions from her husband had been clear. She was to keep Rori away so Marcus could talk to Dr. Sinclair.

Half an hour later, the pair met up with Rori's parents, and the two chefs, at the refreshment table. Marcus handed her a cup of punch and plate full of snacks.

"Eat." His voice brooking no argument. She made a face at him behind his back, not knowing that he could see her reflection in the large mirror behind the refreshment table.

Jess, John and Calvin had joined them just in time to see Marcus catch Rori's nonverbal comeback and saw his secret grin. Marcus shook the young men's hands and gave Jessica a quick hug.

"Thank you," Marcus said to Jessica, his comments including John and Calvin, too.

"For what, Chef?" Jessica asked sweetly, certain he was talking about her conversation with Jake, having confirmed Rori's feelings.

"Clearing things up for me," Marcus said. "I have a favor to ask, though." He continued as she nodded over her cup of punch, "Could you distract Aurora for a few minutes? I need to place a bid on one of her paintings and I don't want her to know."

"Aurora's Castle?"

"Yes," Marcus smiled, "Am I that obvious?"

"Yes!" The trio answered in unison.

Marcus's laughter spoke volumes about the relief that was growing with each passing hour.

Jake, Carla, and Marcus left shortly after. Rori's parents left a few minutes later, offering John, Calvin, and Jessica a ride. Rori would have to stay to give last minute instructions about packaging for the storage company that had been hired for the event. She had no idea how many, if any of her pieces had sold.

Professor Smith waved her over to the auction and cashier's table.

"You did well, tonight," he said. "Looks like only two of your ten pieces will be going with you on Tuesday. Unless, of course, you'd like to donate them to the art department," he hinted broadly.

"We'll see," she laughed. "I'm too tired right now to make a logical decision. "I've got to get home or I'll sleep through graduation." When she got back to the empty apartment, she knew that Jess and John were still out on their date.

She was emotionally drained and totally confused. Marcus had behaved tonight as if nothing had happened at breakfast yesterday. She was too tired to do anything but crawl into bed, so she missed his email saying how much he had enjoyed the show and congratulating her on tomorrow's graduation.

15

Commencement –
The Beginning or the End?

The Masters degree and May undergraduate ceremony was scheduled for ten in the morning. She hated missing church, but it was a long-standing tradition at the secular school. Knowing she had to face Marcus one more time made for more butterflies than expected in the morning.

She donned her white dress and three-inch heels. Her vertically challenged roommate cried foul when she had purchased them for the event.

"That's just cruel!" Jess had protested, "You do not need any more height!"

"But they are the most comfortable ones I've found." She was glad for the extra inches now so she could look Chef High-and-Mighty Charming right in the eyes. Not that I'm going to be able to gather enough courage to do that, but if I do, I'll be prepared!

As the strains of Pomp and Circumstance echoed in the small auditorium, Rori's eyes searched for a tall figure among the line of professors. There were almost as many instructors present as there were graduates.

She saw him, towering above the petite Spanish teacher next to him. Jake was on his other side. This being the smallest graduation of the school year, the instructors traditionally lined their exit path and greeted each of their students. Rori was not looking forward to walking that gauntlet after the ceremony.

Thankfully, the speaker was funny and quite inspirational. And succinct, she was sure her father would add. The professor had endured more boring graduation speakers than he could count. As the graduates filed into the center aisle, their instructors now lining the right side, the realization that this may be the last time she would see Marcus MacRae suddenly dawned on Rori. Fighting tears, she walked past the first few instructors, not having had them for any class. She smiled at one or two she recognized from church or as parents of her school students. The art instructors all greeted her warmly, Professor Smith giving her a big bear hug.

"I'm very proud of you and wish you the best, Aurora," he said sincerely.

"Thank you, Dr. Smith," Rori didn't trust herself to say more. She would miss this school and these people very much.

Facing Marcus was her last obstacle. She was hoping to pass right by him, since technically the class had been an elective, only showing up as a footnote on her transcript. Maybe he wouldn't notice her. No such luck. His hand shot out and stopped her in mid-stride.

"Miss Sinclair?" His eyebrow arched in question. "Did you forget me so quickly?"

"No, Chef MacRae," Rori's stomach flipped. He would laugh to know, or maybe be mad instead, that she had skipped breakfast.

"Congratulations, Princess," he said quietly as he placed a chaste kiss on her cheek and passed her onto to Jake. In the stands, Professor Sinclair was watching intensely.

"Way to go, son," he said quietly.

Jake saw the interchange and the shocked look on Rori's face. He gave her a big hug, hoping to steady her.

"Congrats, brat," he added to snap her back to reality. "We'll see you tomorrow, won't we?" The church had planned a Memorial Day picnic and she had tentative plans to attend, if her packing was mostly done by then. Her parents were leaving early in the morning.

"Hope so," she answered noncommittally as she moved out onto the front lawn to wait for her parents.

As the families and faculty exited the arena, there was no sign of Marcus. Her parents and Jess's family took everyone out to a fancy dinner at the local country club. They all attributed Rori's quietness to the fatigue of the last few days.

The rest of the day was spent packing up Rori's things in the small rental trailer she had rented to accommodate all her art supplies. They said their goodbyes early Monday morning with her dad giving her an enigmatic statement of encouragement.

"Don't be afraid of the future, Princess. And don't forget that our God is an awesomely powerful God who often works in mysterious ways," he said seriously. "Don't be afraid to follow your heart."

Rori checked her email quickly before returning to the little bit of packing she had left. A message from her sister reminded her again of the missed opportunity of her Europe trip. Gwen was preparing for her own graduation and making plans for her new job. The school was an unusual hybrid of a charter school and parochial system, and there were some mandatory training sessions for all new teachers.

Then she saw the familiar name. Still confused over his graduation kiss she wondered what on earth he could possibly want.

Dear Miss Sinclair: Could you please stop by my office sometime this morning? I have some handouts from the last class to give you and some papers I need you to sign. Any time before 11 am, so I can make it to the church picnic. Thank you. ~Chef MacRae.

She looked at the clock. It was a little after nine o'clock. His email had been sent two hours ago. Would he still be there or would he have given up on hearing back from her? And what had happened to the *Marcus* and *Princess Aurora?* Why were we back to *Miss Sinclair* and *Chef MacRae?*

I'll show him, she thought.

Dear Chef Charming: Your wish is my command. I'm on my way. ~Princess Aurora.

Knowing she would never see him again gave her the courage to be petty. Way to go, Rori. Rise to the occasion and show your true colors. She felt guilty for her childish display, but it was too late. The email was on its way.

Instead of making him mad, the message made Marcus laugh and gave him great hope at the same time.

He had stepped out when she arrived. She plopped herself down in one of the worn leather chairs. She was in her faithful painting overalls, planning to spend the morning cleaning out the rest of her art supplies and packing up her car. Knowing now that 'Charming' would be at the picnic, she was considering skipping it.

Coming through the food lab to his office had brought back so many memories. And she could even smell his aftershave in the air. She needed to find out what brand it was so she made sure any future boyfriends stayed away from it. She slumped further into the chair, arms folded, wanting to get whatever torture he had planned over quickly.

Marcus had been standing in the doorway for close to a minute before she realized he was there. Even an untrained eye such as his could read her body language. She was frustrated and wanted to be anywhere but here. And she would have to be wearing those stupid overalls, he thought. She looks about sixteen years old. I feel like a cradle robber. Add that to her hair being down and it's going to take every ounce of self-control to get through this.

"Hello, Aurora," he said quietly, not wanting to startle her too badly. He needed her to trust him, quickly and completely.

"Chef," Rori jumped. "So, I'm here as summoned." Her tone was defensive. His job would be a tough one.

"I'm sorry I startled you," he continued, ignoring her jibe. "You appeared to be deep in thought."

He moved to sit on the edge of his desk, one long leg swinging perilously close to her knee. What is this game he's playing? Rori wondered.

"You said you had some papers for me?" She sat up straighter in the chair trying to put distance between them.

"I have your final handouts and some things I'd like your signature on." Marcus sat where he was, just watching the emotions play across her face. For the first time since he met her, just two weeks ago, he was completely at ease. Normally he felt like a tongue-tied schoolboy with his first crush.

Finally knowing his heart, and having his dreams so close to being fulfilled, gave him unbelievable confidence. Even more importantly, he knew Jake, Carla, and Jess were praying for him and Aurora.

"Well?" Rori was beginning to feel trapped. She did not want to be here but at the same time did not want to leave.

"I know this was just an elective and you were just taking it for fun, but you did do very well." Marcus reached back across his desk and picked up her critique

132

sheet. "Thank you for enduring my lack of manners and bad moods."

"No problem," Rori mumbled, folding the papers and stuffing them into her bag. Her hand brushed against her sketchbook and the humiliation of his sketch came back in a wave. Before she changed her mind, she blurted out, "I'm sorry about the sketch of you in my sketchbook. It was started out of frustration and I should have never kept it. I wish you hadn't seen it."

"No problem," Marcus smiled and mimicked her words and tone, almost identically. How does he do that? She thought. "But actually, I'm glad I saw it. Not only did you capture my natural manliness, your commentary on that particular portion of scripture was spot-on. Perfect description of a stubborn oaf."

"Oh, please," Rori buried her head in her hands. "Don't remind me of my rudeness that night. I was just mad that you were too proud to get into my dumpy little car."

"Aurora Grace," Marcus used the name her father had let slip at the gallery show. "Do you know why I really called you in today?"

"Retribution? Secret torture chamber in the basement? To do an oil portrait for your medieval Scottish mansion?" Rori was grasping at straws emotionally and as normal, her strange and bizarre sense of humor took over.

"Very funny," Marcus moved his large frame to sit directly in front of her chair. Now just resting against the side of the desk, he continued. "I have of couple of things I need to clear up. Did you know that I only read the first two sentences of your sketchbook entry? My reaction was to the picture and your apparent dread of the class, nothing else. Do you understand?"

"You didn't read the whole thing?" Rori was starting to panic.

"Not then," he said.

"Not then?" she echoed his words.

"No," Marcus smiled as she started to understand. "But I have practically memorized it since then."

"Jake." Rori groaned then muttered. "The traitor."

Marcus ignored her and continued, still completely relaxed.

"Secondly, did you know that I spoke at length to your father last night, and again this morning?"

"Is he writing me out of the will?" Rori now felt totally at his mercy. Even if she wanted to escape, she would have to climb over his long legs to get away, or bolt over the back of the chair. Either choice was not very appealing. And for some reason her heart decided to misbehave as it normally did in the presence of Chef Marcus MacRae.

"No," Marcus indulged her verbal horseplay, deciding to turn it against her. "But he's thinking about adding me to it." He watched as Aurora tried to wrap her mind around his meaning.

"He's taking your side over mine?" She had made the only conclusion she would allow her heart to make at this time. "That seems a little unfair after all I've had to put up with the last two weeks."

"Do you really not understand what I'm trying to say to you?" Marcus leaned forward, slightly. Instead of pulling away as he expected, for some reason she appeared to lean towards him also.

"No, I don't," Rori whispered. "You have me totally baffled."

He leaned back abruptly. "Let me put it another way," he folded his arms and leveled his next salvo. "What would you say to some company on your European trip?" The much-loved blush spread across her cheekbones.

"You know someone who can go with me?" She purposely let him think she misunderstood. Surely, he doesn't mean he and I go together? That would be disastrous. Or heavenly.

"Now you are being purposefully obtuse, young lady," Marcus scolded her. "You know exactly what I mean." He unfolded his arms, and in one fluid motion took her hands and pulled her up to face him.

For once, I'm glad I'm tall, Rori thought, only having to tilt her head slightly to look directly into clear green eyes.

"Your father thinks it's a great idea for me to take your sister's place," he continued, "but with one condition."

"Condition?"

"Marry me, Aurora," His simple words hung in the air. "I love you."

"Aurora? Did you hear me?" He rubbed his thumb along the palm of her hand, trying to break the spell. She was simply staring at him, wide-eyed. Was it disbelief or disgust? He couldn't tell and was beginning to worry.

She finally spoke. "You love me?" Tears were forming in her eyes. "I thought you could barely stand me. From the first day of class, everything I did seemed to annoy and irritate you. I don't understand."

"It was a simple and childish defense mechanism," Marcus explained, still only touching her where her hands rested in his. When she continued her silence, he brushed a strand of hair from her cheek, longing to hear her response to his bombshell.

"Oh, Marcus." She buried her head on his chest, crying gentle sobs.

"Why are you crying?" Marcus wrapped his arms around her. "You know that men freak out when women cry, don't you?"

She giggled. "I love you, too, Marcus." She could feel his sigh against her ear. "But I suspect you already knew that, right?"

"The possibility seemed too good to be true, coming only from very biased and decidedly interested observers. I wanted desperately to believe it." He tilted her head back and wiped the tears from her eyes. "Hearing you say it has made my world come completely in focus."

"Princess Aurora Grace Sinclair," Marcus asked in his most serious, gallant tone. "Will you take this poor humble, not-so-charming prince as your husband?"

She answered him with a kiss that was tender but held the promise of a lifetime of love and passion.

"Thank you, Lord," Marcus whispered.

"Amen," Rori smiled.

16
Kiss the Cook

he murmured into her golden locks several minutes later. "About our European trip. I know it's not what most young ladies wish for, a quick wedding that is, but could we possibly make the trip our honeymoon? I'm too old to wait any longer than necessary now that I've found you."

"Absolutely." She smiled and snuggled closer. "No offense to my sister, but that sounds so much more inviting than what I had originally planned."

"I have a confession," Marcus said as he gently broke away from Aurora's embrace. He swallowed hard at the sight of her languid eyes and the sound of her innocent sigh.

"What?" Rori asked, still half in a dreamy fog. "Are you really a Scottish prince and I'll have to go live in a faraway castle or are you a frog under a spell that turns you into a handsome prince?"

"No such luck, Princess." He pulled her out of the privacy of his office, led her down the hall and into the brightness of the afternoon sun.

"Where are we going?"

"That's part of the confession." A slightly guilty look crossed his face. "All your stuff is at my place."

"At your place?"

"Yes." His grin widened as he watched her quick mind make the jump to the only logical conclusion.

"Awfully sure of yourself, weren't you?" She stopped and yanked her hand loose from his. Her mock indignation accented by folded arms and a tapping foot.

"Well," Marcus had the wisdom to at least act a little humble, and then proceeded to defend himself. "It was your father's idea!"

"Oh, really?" Rori was laughing now as they continued down the block to his apartment building.

"Before we go up, I have a call to make," Marcus said as he stopped in the lobby and dialed Jake's number.

"Well?" Jake asked anxiously, "What did she say? The suspense is killing us here!"

Marcus could almost see Carla's dark curls bouncing as he heard her in the background, "Tell us!"

"Yes," Marcus laughed. "She said yes." He held the phone up so Aurora could hear the screams of delight. He loved how she blushed. Life with this woman was going to be a sweet adventure.

Turning back to Jake, Marcus continued. "Could you guys stop by in a few minutes? We might need help arranging some boxes."

Jake laughed. "Yeah, how did she react to that little trick?"

"Still pretending to be mad, I think," Marcus winked at Rori as she rolled her eyes. Jake promised to bring Carla and Zoe over in a few minutes, since they lived just a couple streets away. He, John Liu, and Calvin had all helped unload the trailer Rori's dad had covertly brought by early this morning.

Unlocking the door of his unit, Marcus stepped in front of Rori. His look was serious and she watched him intently, her eyes wide.

"I didn't imagine it, did I?" he asked quietly apprehensive. "You did say yes, right?"

Rori smiled and nodded. His nervous question would surprise most people that knew this lion of a man. Then, just as quickly as his serious tone had come, it disappeared. He scooped her up in his arms and kicked open his door.

"Your castle, my lady," he said as he carried her over the threshold.

"I love how you've decorated the place," she giggled, looking at the mound of boxes and art supplies plopped unceremoniously in the middle of his living room. Knowing how neat he normally was, this was probably driving him crazy, she thought.

"Very funny," Marcus said as he set her down on one of the stacks of boxes and kissed her soundly. He had promised himself to enjoy all the affection he could steal today, with the assurance that Jake and his family would be here soon to keep his attentions in check. He valued his integrity too much to let his desire for this woman ruin their reputations. It's going to be a long four weeks, though, he thought.

They discussed her having the second bedroom as a studio, unless she wanted to rent a space at the Downtown Gallery, or even at the school, as Professor Smith had mentioned to Marcus earlier that morning while helping stash Rori's art supplies.

"Dr. Smith was in on this too?" Rori asked. "Was I the only one in the dark?"

"Well," Marcus said, sheepishly. "I didn't want you to have to move your art supplies home and then back again. Dr. Smith graciously overlooked the fact that I had been skulking around the art studio last week and seemed genuinely pleased to help my little adventure."

"You were skulking?" Rori laughed. "Is that anything like stalking?" As she teased him, she looked around the extra bedroom. It had a large window that offered plenty of light and would be perfect for a studio. As they came back into the living room, Rori stopped suddenly.

"That's my painting!" She was staring at *Aurora's Castle* now proudly displayed over the fireplace. "You bid on it?"

"Of course I did." Marcus smiled, proud that he had surprised her. "I'm glad I won it outright, because if I hadn't, I would have had to hunt down the winner and uh…" he hesitated for emphasis, "persuade them to sell it to me."

"Jess teased me mercilessly about it, you know," Rori said, shyly giving Marcus a quick kiss of thanks. "She insisted you were the whole motivation behind it. I don't have any idea where she got such an idea," Rori said facetiously. "It's not like I started it right after I met you or anything."

Their helpers arrived soon and all her possessions were stored quickly, and neatly, in the extra bedroom. Carla, Zoe, and Rori went back to her dorm so she could change.

"Were you surprised?" Carla's excitement was evident. "We couldn't be happier. You are just what Marcus needs. He gets so serious sometimes and I knew right away that something was going on when he talked about you after the first cooking class. I hadn't seen him that relaxed since culinary school when he and Jake got into all sorts of scrapes."

When the girls met up with the men at the picnic, Rori had changed from her overalls into a cute light green and blue shorts set. Marcus would have preferred the overalls, but he kept his opinion to himself. He was grateful that she had pulled her hair back into a ponytail.

Rori was not looking forward to leaving the next morning. She would head home for Gwen's graduation and now to find a wedding dress. She and Marcus, along with Carla, Jake, and Jessica, had talked long into the night about wedding plans. In truth, the ladies had talked, the guys had listened in-between innings of the baseball game.

The wedding being less than four weeks away actually made planning much easier. The ceremony would be a small affair with mainly family and a few close friends. At the picnic, they had talked to Sam and he was thrilled to clear his schedule on that Saturday evening to perform the service. The church had a lovely gazebo and gardens that were available for church members. They stopped by Sam's office before heading home to reserve it on the church calendar.

Even just one day into their engagement, everything seemed to be falling into place. Still, Rori was worried.

"I'm still afraid I'm going to wake up tomorrow and this is all going to have been a fabulous dream," Rori admitted to Carla as she placed the toy tiara that hung over her bed on Zoe's dark curls.

"You know, Rori," Carla said, sounding much older and wiser than her years. "You do have to trust that God loves you enough to bless you even beyond your wildest dreams."

The next morning Rori's car was packed and Marcus had met her for an early breakfast before his class started. He was teaching a two-week intensive for the year-round culinary students in addition to another community cooking class.

"This is going to be the longest four weeks of my life," he said as he hugged Rori close one more time.

Rori just nodded, snuggling closer, unwilling to give up the security of his embrace. When she woke up that morning, she had to get assurance from Jessica that yesterday's events had really happened.

"Yes," her sleepy roommate had replied. "You and Chef Charming are engaged. It was all very romantic."

Despite her sarcasm, Jessica was actually very, very happy for Rori. She had insisted that Rori wake her up to say goodbye before heading home.

Now nestled in his arms, Rori sighed. Her hands were resting on Marcus' chest and she could feel his heart beating. Finally, Marcus pushed her gently away. He tilted her face up with a finger under her chin and kissed her.

"You've got to get on the road." He rubbed his thumb along her jaw line. "And I've got to get to class." She merely nodded, eyes still closed, hoping for another kiss.

"Aurora, look at me," her fiancé commanded. She smiled impishly, aware she was dragging out the goodbye.

"I'll call you tonight, but it might be late," Marcus reminded her. "My community class starts tonight and it's scheduled to go half an hour later that yours did, to make up for missing Memorial Day."

"Or you could just email me." Rori grinned. "That worked well in the past."

He opened her car door and buckled her seat belt using the motion as an excuse to grab one more kiss.

"That may happen occasionally," he said, now leaning through the window after closing her door. "But I know I'll need to hear your voice every day, too. Call it an addiction."

Rori boldly ran her fingers through his hair, needing one last physical connection. Marcus' breath caught and he jerked away.

"Behave, woman," he admonished.

"I love you," she said almost pleadingly, wishing he hadn't been so eager to break away.

"I love you, too," he stated in a no-nonsense manner. "Now off with you! Call me and leave a message that you've arrived safely, ok?" He leaned in for one last kiss.

"Yes, Lord Marcus," she said sassily as she started her car.

Hoping to catch him the next morning before his class began, Rori got up early and grabbed her phone. She opened her email app, knowing he was most likely prepping for his morning class.

Dear Marcus, I'm sorry I was asleep when you called. I know I probably didn't make much sense. How were your classes? No lovely young women?

He obviously was at his computer as he sent a message almost immediately.

I loved the sound of your voice, just awake from sleep, he typed, the backspaced deleting what he had just typed, deciding that statement was probably crossing the line that he had laid out in his mind for his own, and her, protection. He began again.

I know that the last two weeks were crazy for you and you need to catch up on your rest. You sounded quite cute, if slightly incoherent. Classes went well, and you do not need to worry. There are three happily married couples, the husbands having apparently lost a bet (from what I could tell), two grumpy old codgers, two middle-aged sisters, and two older ladies. One of the ladies is a volunteer at the high school cafeteria and the other is her recently widowed neighbor. Should be a good class. Of course, nowhere near as exciting as last time.

Or as life changing, he thought.

That's reassuring, but I still can't help being a little jealous. They get to see you every day. I miss you. What time will you be here on Friday?

He smiled at her enthusiasm.

Sweet Aurora– I miss you, too. I plan to be there early on Friday, probably before nine. Jake must be extremely excited about all this for him to volunteer to cover my Friday and Saturday classes. Speaking of classes, I hear the herd approaching. I love you, Princess.

17
A Rival Prince

Her sister called over her shoulder as she opened the door to her tall handsome soon-to-be brother-in-law. "Rori, Marcus is here!"

Marcus was nervous. He had spent the two-hour trip from campus to the Sinclair hometown with prayers and mental planning. Although he had spent several hours just last weekend discussing his feelings and plans with Rori's dad, now that they were officially engaged, things were different. Plus, Marcus had forgotten what life before Aurora Sinclair was like and the last four days had been miserable.

"Marcus!" Rori practically launched herself into his arms from the stairs that were just to his right. She had been on her way downstairs already when her sister called. Her exuberance was both intoxicating and embarrassing to the normally reticent Scottish man.

"You're embarrassing him, Rori," he heard her mother call from the kitchen. "Let him at least get in the door."

"Sorry," she giggled against his neck. "You can put me down now." Marcus dropped her quickly. He had caught her mid-jump and had her dangling inches off the floor. He flushed bright red.

"You scamp," he whispered good-naturedly in her ear. "I'm trying to make a good impression."

"Welcome son," Professor Sinclair shook his hand after Rori pulled him into the dining room. "I hope you're ready for a crazy couple of days. You mention wedding to a household of women and you might as well go and hide because madness will ensue."

"I'm ready, sir," Marcus replied and added, "If I could get away with eloping tonight I would." The knowing look from the older man gave him the impression that Rori's father understood and completely agreed. As Dr. Sinclair motioned for them to retreat to the back deck, Marcus could tell there was something else the older man wanted to say.

"I need to tell you about Jason," her father's tone indicated the seriousness of the upcoming conversation.

"Jason?"

"There was a boy in high school that had a devastating effect on my daughter. It was over six years ago, but I sometimes have to remind myself that I've forgiven him."

Marcus braced himself for what sounded like a troubling story but knew from Dr. Sinclair's tone that it must be important.

"Jason was a popular football player and Rori, despite how she looks now, back then she was a gawky, skinny teenager with untamed hair and glasses. She never seemed concerned about her looks, although she wasn't sloppy or unkempt, just didn't fit into the popular group.

Apparently, Jason and some friends concocted a scheme to see who could get Rori to agree to go out with them, with the ultimate plan of standing her up and making her disgrace known throughout school."

Marcus's anger was searing at this point. Her dad continued.

"For some reason, Rori had developed a schoolgirl crush on Jason and he knew it. She was so excited when he asked her out that the happiness transformed her. She came down the morning of her date, having borrowed a stylish outfit from a friend and even venturing to try the contacts we had ordered for her several months before. She looked like a different girl. She was still floating on a cloud after school and was ready for her date almost an hour early."

Dr. Sinclair hesitated noticeably. "Jason never came. I remember holding her that night while she cried herself to sleep."

The pain was evident in the father's voice and Marcus was battling the urge to hunt the young man down and inflict physical pain for the emotional pain he caused Rori.

"What she didn't know until later is that I called the young man the next morning. I also spoke to his father. Jason seemed distraught, but his father was furious. The young man dropped off the football team, supposedly for health reasons, and within a few weeks had transferred to the local private school."

Marcus was again in awe of Rori's father. His wisdom, both in handling the situation through Jason's father, and in not telling Rori what he had done, was inspiring.

"Rori recovered quicker than I expected, at least outwardly. The new look she wore to school that day had helped soften the blow of the humiliation. Jason's dad, with Jason's help, made sure that rumors swirled implying that she was the one who had rejected his son. I'm still amazed at the integrity of that boy's father. We didn't hear from Jason again until almost two years later. He called and asked if he could talk to Rori when she was home from college one weekend. I made sure Rori was okay with the idea. It was then that we found out that her recovery was just outward. She panicked at the thought of seeing him as the feelings of humiliation resurfaced. She hadn't dated or even been interested in anyone since then. It took some convincing and prayer, but she finally agreed to see him."

"You let him see her again?" Marcus interrupted, glad the scoundrel was not within reach, sure he would do Jason bodily harm.

"It worked out well, trust me," Professor Sinclair said, glad to see Marcus ready to defend his daughter. "Jason had experienced a huge crisis of faith and had completely turned his life around. He apologized to Rori and begged forgiveness. He even admitted that he had tried to get out of the bet because he really did like Rori even before her outward transformation. 'I shouldn't have been so concerned with my so-called friends,' Jason told her, 'I was a stupid, ignorant, wicked, fool.' She agreed with his self-assessment but did eventually forgive him. I know now how deeply the incident had hurt her because it wasn't until after that meeting that we recovered the Rori we know now. It was like a weight had been lifted."

"Thank you, Dr. Sinclair," Marcus said quietly. "I am feeling overwhelmed, but I know that is an important piece of the intricate puzzle that is Aurora. I'll admit that it frightens me a little when I realize how much I don't know about my future wife."

"But Marcus," Rori's dad comforted him with a laugh. "That's part of the fun of being married!"

As the two men came back inside, they discussed the plans for the weekend, knowing they were both at the mercy of the ladies.

"Rori's mom has started a list of decisions that only you two need to make and I think Rori wants you to go look at flowers and wedding rings," her father said. "You guys are free this evening, too, since Mrs. Sinclair and I will be taking Rori's sister out for her graduation dinner."

"That will be nice," Marcus admitted. "I have a little surprise planned that I hope will work out. I have a friend from culinary school that has a restaurant downtown. I'm hoping to get in between lunch and dinner service and introduce him to Aurora."

"You two are going over to your parent's house on Saturday evening, correct?" the professor asked. Marcus's family lived about an hour away.

"Yes," Marcus said. "They're eager to meet Aurora and we need to get my grandmother's engagement ring on her finger!" Rori's dad laughed at the obvious enthusiasm.

"We're also scheduled to meet with our family pastor for pre-marital counseling," Marcus added. "He's a friend of the pastor back home and they're going to tag-team our counseling sessions."

"I'm glad you two are fitting that in even though time is short," Dr. Sinclair said. "It's always good to be aware of the possible pitfalls early in a marriage and starting with a good foundation is very important."

"We've made those sessions a priority, but we're going to try to fit all the other traditional wedding plans in also," Marcus said. "I know our engagement has been unconventional, but I don't want Rori to miss out on any of the fun most brides get to experience. Although, I must say again that elopement is a tempting option."

"Avoiding the frenzy of the next month is an appealing thought," Dr. Sinclair said. "But I'm afraid that would only add to the raised eyebrows you two have already experienced. Am I correct?"

"Yes," Marcus said with a frown. "I'd appreciate any advice on how to combat the expected questions. I want to protect Rori as much as I can."

"As do I," Rori's dad said. The older man was impressed with this young man's integrity. "The fact that both families, your friends, her friends, and everyone that cares about you two, all are thrilled with the idea, is essential."

"I will admit that has been a huge comfort," Marcus said, smiling as he thought of Jake and Carla's whole-hearted support.

"The best advice I can give you is something that will also help quiet any critics," the wise man continued. "Marcus, don't argue with God's timing."

Marcus stared at Rori's father. The simple words had left the nervous groom-to-be with a surprising sense of peace.

"Thank you, sir," he said. "That is exactly what I needed to hear."

After their quick coffee and breakfast, Marcus and Rori headed out to tackle their list. She was simply looking forward to spending time with him and was finding it hard to care much about the details. She was looking forward to finding her dress, which she had grand plans to do early next week.

Sitting next to him in his car, Rori wished he would hold her hand, but he needed both to drive the manual transmission car. She resisted the urge to run her fingers along his forearms, almost embarrassing herself with the direction of her thoughts. Who would have thought strong, masculine arms could be so sexy? She knew her experience on the first night of class when Marcus had held her hands to demonstrate the cutting technique was responsible for her fascination.

"You're awfully quiet, Princess," Marcus squeezed her hand as they sat at a red light. "What are you thinking about?"

She blushed. "You wouldn't believe me if I told you."

"Try me."

"Nope. It's embarrassing."

He raised his eyebrows inquiringly.

"Really," she insisted. "I'll tell you when we're married."

"That bad, huh?"

The rest of the morning was productive. They found matching trinity knot rings that paid homage to his Scottish heritage and her English-Irish roots. Trying them on made the seriousness of what they were doing a reality. Rori caught Marcus watching her intently in the mirror behind the counter. She smiled as he mouthed, 'I love you.'

As he held the door to his car for her after they left the jeweler's, Marcus pulled her close and kissed her quickly but effectively. She rewarded him with a contented sigh.

"I'm very impressed, Chef." Rori complimented him as they sat among a rainbow of flowers at their next stop. "You seem to be enjoying this."

"It's an act," he tried to deny he was thoroughly enjoying watching his fiancée surrounded by her flower choices. "I really don't know the difference between a carnation and a peony. I do like the irises, though," he said, pointing to the deep purple stems that Rori had placed on her favorites list.

"Good," Rori said. "Because that's what we're using. I think everything else just doesn't look like us."

"So, we're done?" Marcus asked, trying to hide his hopeful tone.

"Yes, Mr. Impatient," she laughed. "What would you like to do now? The only other thing we absolutely have to get done this weekend is the invitation list. With the culinary department doing the light supper after the ceremony, we are in great shape. The only thing easier would have been eloping."

Marcus groaned inwardly. The thought of eloping and making her his wife quicker than the already hasty four weeks was more tempting than she should know.

"My mother, and yours, would never speak to us again if we eloped," he reminded her, trying to hide his true feelings.

"I know," she laughed again. "At least it's going to be a small family affair. I don't think I would like a big wedding." Plus, I don't want to wait that long she added mentally but didn't want to admit such a provocative thought to him.

"Are you hungry?" Marcus had called his friend while Rori was looking at flowers in the back room with the florist. Jose was thrilled to hear from his old friend and was more than pleased to share his kitchen this afternoon. Their lunch service was over in a half hour and dinner prep wouldn't start for another couple of hours.

"Umm, yes," Rori said. "What did you have in mind?"

"It's a surprise."

18

A Nervous Princess

Their afternoon turned out to be one of the most enjoyable times Rori had ever had. Chef Jose Ramirez regaled her with tales of Jake and Marcus in school. The two chefs even let her participate in the preparation of their meal. While she wasn't chopping vegetables, she sat on a stool out of their way and sketched.

"Wow, you're good!" Jose said as he looked over her shoulder. She had sketched the two chefs intensely bent over a sumptuous plate of food. "Can you sign it and let me put it up on the wall?"

She laughed and complied. Rori was always amazed that people liked her art, especially the pieces that took such little time.

The three enjoyed their meal as the couple described their unconventional courtship to the chef.

"Way to go, big guy," Jose thumped Marcus on the back. "Didn't know you had it in you!"

"Thanks for the vote of confidence, buddy," Marcus laughed.

"Hey, Rori," Jose said as they left the restaurant, "if you change your mind, call me."

"Not likely, but thanks for the offer." She gave him a quick kiss on the cheek.

"You are one lucky guy, Marcus," Jose told his friend. "Take care of that lovely lady."

"I will." Marcus thought that the next three weeks were going to be the longest of his life. His love for this fascinating woman deepened with each new experience they shared.

Later that evening, sitting in the family den, Marcus knew Rori was working on her resume online, so he opened his email program and quickly typed.

Dearest Aurora, you are gorgeous and I love you.

He knew immediately when she got the message even though no one else in the room would have known. Her slightly raised eyebrow gave it away.

Really? You're sending me a message from across the room? Rori answered in the message box.

Yes, couldn't resist the urge and didn't want to disturb the family. He knew a text would draw attention from the family. Rori's dad was dutifully, but reluctantly looking at wedding announcement examples with his enthusiastic wife. Gwen was working through the classroom requirements for the new charter school.

You are silly, Aurora responded.

You've rubbed off on me. Not sure anyone would've called me 'silly' three weeks ago.

It's just because they didn't know you very well.

I've found some Bible verses we could use in the ceremony. I'm going to forward them to you, okay?

Or, I could just come over there, Rori offered, really looking for an excuse to sit next to him.

Marcus saw her bite her lip as she typed. He forced himself to look away.

No. I'm also sending you an email with the preliminary menu from the culinary guys. The real reason he wanted her to stay put was that the temptation was too great. It was reasonable to be attracted to his future wife, but he had resolved to protect the precious gift God had dropped unexpectedly into his life. To soften his rejection, he added, *Plus, if I kiss you like I want to, it would embarrass your parents.* Rori giggled.

Thankfully, her mom chose that moment to call them up to the dining room to look at the wedding invitation examples, interrupting their secret message session. At least they thought it was secret. Donnie Sinclair had watched the interchange between the couple as they pretended to ignore each other. When he heard Marcus tell Rori to behave as they headed to the dining room, he realized he needed to have one more conversation with Marcus.

"Before you join the ladies, I need to mention one last thing, Marcus," Donnie Sinclair said. "It's a touchy subject, but I won't dance around the topic. I know a short engagement has several benefits. I was once your age, engaged to Rori's mom, and I know all the temptations that come with that situation."

Marcus nodded. "Obviously, you've developed mind-reading skills. Please tell me it's not genetic."

Donnie laughed. "No, just experience," he said. "As you probably have surmised, Rori has little experience with men. She's obviously head over heels in love with you, and her natural exuberance might place you in the position of being the one that protects you both."

"Absolutely," Marcus said. "I've already seen the need to…discourage Rori's affections. As difficult as that is, I've come to realize she has no idea the power she has over me."

"They do have tremendous power, don't they? Be aware, they always will. It's not always a negative thing, though." Donnie encouraged Marcus with a grin. "And you're correct. I'm sure Rori is unaware of the effect her flirting has."

"You'll have to walk a very thin line. If you allow her—and yourself—too much freedom, you may find yourself easily compromised. I know you don't want to start your marriage with that burden, and you understand that would greatly disappoint her mother and me as well as your parents, I'm sure."

"Understood," Marcus said and turned to leave.

"I'm not sure you do understand," Rori's father continued, "at least not completely. This may sound contradicting, but there's a danger in moving too far the other direction on the spectrum, too. From what I've observed you're doing well, but as the wedding gets closer, her fears may start surfacing. There will be a danger of her interpreting any resistance to affection as a sign of doubt on your part."

Donnie watched his words take effect. It was obvious they had connected with Marcus. He sent the younger man on his way with a word of encouragement. "From our perspective, we're thrilled that she has such an exceptional object for her attentions."

Late Saturday afternoon, Marcus and Rori arrived at his parent's house. His mom and dad were thrilled with Rori, realizing immediately this vivacious, merry soul was a perfect match for their son. Mrs. MacRae had already spent time on the phone with Rori's mom, and her plans were in full swing. Marcus and his dad left the ladies to the wedding details and headed out to the deck to talk.

"Have you told her about Carissa yet?" His dad asked. Carissa was Marcus's college girlfriend. They had dated exclusively for several months, but thankfully, Marcus had realized she was not as serious about her faith as he was. Their breakup was not pleasant and he had only been on very casual dates since then, almost four years ago.

"No," Marcus realized he had forgotten about Carissa. "I really haven't thought about her in months, and definitely not in the last three weeks."

"You might want to bring it up," his dad advised, "Maybe in your session with Pastor Jay tomorrow after church."

In the living room, Marcus's sister had pulled out the family photo albums and Rori was enjoying seeing

Marcus as a child and young man. As she turned the page, she heard his mom whisper to her daughter.

"Here, Rori," Katie said, reaching for the album. "Let's look at these later. I know Mother is anxious to get these lists done." Her obvious interruption was too late. Rori was staring at a formal picture of Marcus and a gorgeous petite brunette.

"Who's this?" Rori forgot her resolve to be dainty and ladylike when she was with Marcus's family. The distressed curiosity was evident in her voice.

"Just an old girlfriend," Mrs. MacRae explained. "Carissa and Marcus dated in college. It didn't end well."

"We didn't really like her," Katie interjected. "She was snooty and I think she just went to church with us to keep her hooks in him."

"Kathryn Lynn MacRae!" her mother scolded.

"Well, it's true," the young woman tried to look apologetic. Their banter had given Rori time to recover. The woman in the picture was gorgeous and so completely her opposite that she was immediately distraught. She wanted to run and hide but instead used humor to cover her feelings.

"Well, we'll have to cross that name off the baby names list, won't we?" Rori quipped, forcing herself to grin as she closed the photo album and handed it to Katie.

Mrs. MacRae and Katie joined in her laughter, relieved that their soon to be family member was not easily upset. They had no idea that Rori was in fact dying inside. She knew she would never be able to compete with the beauty in the photograph.

Marcus assumed her quietness that evening was just due to the pace of the wedding planning. She was sharing a room with Katie and he pulled his sister aside and instructed her to make sure they didn't stay up late talking. Rori needed her rest.

"She found out about Carissa this afternoon," Katie informed him.

"What?" Marcus almost growled. "What were you thinking?"

"Don't yell at me!" Katie stood her ground. "Rori took it all in stride. She said something about making sure Carissa was marked off the potential baby names list. She is really special, big brother."

"Yes, she is," Marcus said, mentally trying to decide how to bring up the subject with Rori. "Do you think I should say something to her?"

"I don't know," Katie said with her wise nineteen years of experience. "Maybe you should. It probably would have been better coming from you."

"Thanks, baby sister," Marcus hugged her and gave her a quick kiss on the forehead.

"Wow," Katie said quietly, unused to outward displays of affection from either older brother. Must be Rori's influence, she thought. I like it!

Sunday morning dawned with a misty welcome. Rori followed the aroma of coffee downstairs to find Marcus was the only one awake. He took advantage of the opportunity and gave her a long hug.

"Did you sleep well?" he asked breathing in the lavender scent of her hair. He kissed her lightly, not trusting himself with anymore, and released her.

"Yes," Rori smiled. He thought the smile was a little false, but just accredited his doubts with the newness of their relationship. He was anxious to become familiar with her ever-changing expressions.

She was looking forward to the worship service, hoping that the hymns and message would help her troubled heart. Although their family church was more formal than the church she and Marcus attended just off campus, the teaching was solid and the songs familiar. She left the service with a lighter heart. They grabbed a quick fast-food meal before returning to meet with the Pastor.

Having so little time to fit in pre-marital counseling the couple had arranged for this meeting and two meetings with Pastor Sam back home. Understanding their different personalities was the aim of today's session. A lot of laughter and teasing ensued, which encouraged Pastor Lawrence.

These two were opposites in many ways, but surprisingly held strong convictions about child-rearing, finances, and the importance of their spiritual lives. Confident that they could work through the inevitable conflicts that arose from being male and female, the pastor encouraged them. Although one of them was extremely organized and controlled and one lived life from moment to moment, he pointed out that if they loved and respected each other and learned to appreciate the other's viewpoint, these differences would actually make for a very complete and stable marriage.

"Major on the major, and minor on the minor," the pastor left them with his best piece of advice.

Stories of Marcus as a child filled the conversation at the family dinner early that evening. Rori couldn't help but laugh, despite the shadow that still clung to her when she thought about his old girlfriend. She tried to shake off the doubts.

On their drive back to Rori's home, Marcus mentioned Carissa.

"I hear that you were unexpectedly informed about the infamous Carissa," he carefully broached the subject. "You do know that she was never, ever as important to me as you are, right? Even from the first moment I saw you, I think all thoughts or memories of her faded completely away. Honestly when my dad suggested that I mention her to you, my first thought was, 'Who is Carissa?'

"Thank you, Charming," Rori sighed, leaned over and kissed him quickly on the cheek. She knew that he probably thought he had erased all her doubts, but Rori could still picture the gorgeous, petite brunette smiling up at him in the photographs. This is my problem, not his, though, she decided. I'll have to make it a prayer priority.

Marcus dropped her back at her parent's house and after a quick cup of coffee, prepared to head back home. Rori walked him to the car, her family giving the couple a few minutes of privacy.

"Princess," Marcus held her hands lightly. "I love you."

"I love you, too, Marcus," Rori wanted Marcus to hold her close and kiss away her questions, but he seemed content to let the cool evening breeze swirl between them. He finally pulled her close and kissed her softly.

"I've got to go," he whispered against her hair. "I'll call you when I get home."

"Okay." She waited in the driveway until his car turned out of the neighborhood.

Monday night Rori emailed Marcus timing it just as his evening class should be ending, hoping he had turned his notifications on his phone back on. He had.

Marcus, you should be very, very thankful.

I am, but remind me again, why? His message instantly popped up.

You are marrying a very unusual woman.

Again, I agree, but what specific characteristic are you classifying as unusual? I can think of several.

I hate shopping especially trying on clothes – yuck! That will save you a lot of money in the long run.

Marcus wasn't surprised. Rori was not an ordinary woman.

That bad today, huh? **He** was tempted to add, *"We could elope...."* but resisted the urge.

It's funny, but I enjoyed trying on wedding gowns, which was surprising. I felt very princess-like.

Marcus groaned. You are killing me. Please, Lord, I'm struggling again here. He remembered once again the conversation he had with her father. It was clear she had no idea how she affected him. He tried to make his response as nonchalant as possible.

Did you find one?

Not 'the' one yet. I kept sending Jess pictures so she could give input and that helped. I did find a couple that I really liked. Mom and I are going to one more place tomorrow or Monday.

Any chance I could get a picture?

No way.

A description?

Not a chance.

Hints?

Nope.

You are a cruel, cruel woman. He could picture her playful grin as their conversation continued.

Yes sir. It's payback.

Payback?

Oops, Rori realized she had just headed down a secret road. Oh well, here goes nothing.

Yes, payback. Since you insist on wearing your kilt and I have to suffer through the ceremony being totally distracted, you can suffer a few days wondering what my dress will look like.

My kilt? Distraction? I'm lost. I thought you liked the idea. If you don't, you need to let me know so Dad, James, and I can figure something else out.

No, no. Kilts are fine.

Then the problem is...?

I love the idea, (I'm only telling you this since we're not face–to–face). Your long, muscular legs are extremely attractive. Now, I'm going now, mortifyingly embarrassed, but deeply in love with you, Lord Marcus – Aurora

Silly girl, you have made me laugh. I love you.

Not trusting a simple text would adequately convey her excitement, she called Marcus on Wednesday and left a message on his phone.

"I found a dress!"

A long day of classes meant his response arrived much later that evening.

Your phone message could be classified as cruel and unusual punishment, Marcus texted.

Sorry, but it's really, really pretty, Rori explained.

Even meaner, Marcus stated.

Sorry, I'll stop, Rori conceded.

I love you, Aurora.

I love you, too, Marcus. I started another countdown in my sketchbook. Seventeen days.

I hope my picture is better on this one! Marcus remembered the caricature she had drawn and how mad he was when he first saw it. Looking back now, he knew the picture in the sketchbook was what pushed him to admit his feelings for Aurora Grace Sinclair and had convinced him not to give up hope.

What do you mean? The first one. was very credible.

Imp! Life with this woman was going to be a joy.

19
Doubt and Dilemma

Early the following Friday morning, Rori, her mom, and Mrs. MacRae were heading towards the campus. They were planning to spend the weekend checking on the dinner arrangements and final details. They also both wanted a look at the gazebo and gardens where the wedding was to take place.

The two very organized and motivated mothers made the potentially hectic plans flow like a well-oiled machine. As far as plans and details went, their wedding was a dream. Rori only wished her emotions were as undisturbed.

Rori was glad that their chatter filled the car so neither lady noticed her silence. She and Marcus had talked each evening, but he was busy with the community cooking class. Even though he was co-teaching the intensive class for the culinary students with Jake, it still took up a lot a time. He was usually exhausted when they were finally able to speak each evening. Plus, she didn't feel confident enough anymore to burden him with her doubts. She knew he would probably say she was ridiculous for worrying.

The moms had rented a hotel room, but Rori was staying with Carla and Zoe. Jess was coming over later to make it a fun girl's night. Jake had been booted out to spend the weekend with Marcus.

After dropping the ladies off at the hotel, Rori met Carla at the Marcus's condominium, which had been designated as the collection point for wedding supplies. They were planning to spend the morning on party favors. Carla noticed Rori's unusual quietness.

"What's wrong?" Carla knew something was bothering her friend.

"Nothing, just tired," Rori explained. She forced herself into a more cheerful mood, and apparently was convincing enough. Carla let the matter drop, but was still concerned.

"I didn't think it would make such a mess," Rori exclaimed over the disaster facing Marcus when he came home to find her and Carla in his kitchen. He was exhausted from the week of classes and nervous about the wedding. The stress made him short-tempered. Unfortunately, Jake was not here to warn him of the dangerous ground ahead.

"Exactly," he grumbled. "You didn't think." Moving their wedding craft project off his kitchen counter impatiently. His back was facing her so he didn't see the blood drain from her face. Carla did but was unable to stop Rori before she bolted out the back door.

"You big, dumb idiot," Carla pounded her small fists on his back.

"What?" Marcus turned, trying to fend off the surprise attack.

"She's gone!" Carla pointed out the sliding glass door. "I can't believe you just said that to her! She practically worships you, and you just questioned her intelligence. How could you? Especially knowing about how she was treated by what's-his-name, that jerk in high school. You fool!"

"Jason," Marcus said as his conversation with Rori's father came flooding back. He had shared a brief version of it with Jake and Carla over breakfast that morning.

"What have I done?" Marcus felt a yawning pit of despair open up beneath him.

"Go after her you doofus!" Carla's vocabulary seemed to have an endless supply of words to describe his stupidity.

Marcus found Rori curled up on the bench swing hanging in the gazebo at the edge of the community park. He knelt beside her and reached out to brush the hair from her face.

"Please don't touch me." Her words conveyed the depth of her hurt. "I'm fine. I knew you would change your mind. Can you please just get this over with so I don't have to face public humiliation again? I don't think I'll survive this one."

"Change my mind?" Marcus asked, "What the h..., heck would I change my mind about?" His emotions running so high, he was in danger of slipping into colorful speech.

Rori lifted her head slightly, eyebrows raised and bright blue eyes peeking over her folded arms. He knew she was reacting to his choice, or almost choice, of words.

"Sorry," he muttered. "What have I changed my mind about, if you will please enlighten me?" He was angry with himself but Rori assumed his tone was still directed at her.

"Loving me."

He stood abruptly and moved to the bench next to her perch. The normally controlled, stoic man fought for control but a glance at the dejected young woman before him brought tears to his eyes.

"Aurora," Marcus pleaded. "Look at me. Please."

She raised her head again. He could see her blue eyes, brilliant in the evening light. Surprisingly, they held no tears, just a haunted look.

"I love you. I will always love you. Nothing you can do will ever, ever change that." She rolled her eyes and buried her head on her arms again.

"Whatever." The bitterness was harder to take than anger. He moved back to her side and in one motion lifted her from the swing. He settled himself in the spot where she had been sitting and cradled her in his arms.

She was amazed at how easily he lifted her. Being as tall as she was meant she had never felt dainty. Until now. Still her long legs combined with his not-so-small frame, made for a very close proximity in the swing.

"I am an idiot. I should never have said what I did." Marcus apologized, knowing that it was probably too little and too late. "I have no excuse but that I'm tired and nervous and I want the wedding to be here already."

She shrugged her shoulders slightly. He was desperate to get through to her.

"You are so different from me that it makes me crazy with envy sometimes. I wish I could just go with the flow and enjoy life like you do. You're going to have to help me loosen up and you have my permission to wallop me when I get on one of my rampages."

"You're jealous of me?" Marcus caught his breath as she lifted her head. Her breath against his neck was very distracting.

"Yes."

"I'm sorry I messed up your kitchen. You want everything to stay neat and orderly and I'm not sure I can do that. So, it is okay if you want to change your mind. I'll understand."

"If you don't marry me, I think I'll go insane." Marcus stated his case succinctly. "Aurora, I need to know that you forgive me," Marcus whispered, his lips against her ear. "I'm a fool. I love you more than life itself."

"I forgive you," Rori sighed Marcus could feel her relax as she snuggled against him. Something she said still bothered him. He needed to understand what was going through the busy mind of the woman in his arms.

"What did you mean by facing public humiliation," he asked, "*again*?"

"Nothing," Rori's breath against his chest was distracting. Marcus tilted her chin up.

"Tell me," Marcus said. "I want to understand." Having to push months of conversations into four weeks had been difficult. Marcus knew this point was crucial. Rori just shook her head. Deciding that bringing up the awful memory was better than not knowing, Marcus pushed her.

"Jason?" he asked. He saw the brief cringe before it was buried again. She shrugged her shoulders. "What did your father not tell me?"

"Daddy didn't know," Rori said. She tried to push her way out her fiancé's embrace. The humiliation and shame came rushing back.

"Didn't know what?" Marcus held her away from him slightly, but did not let her leave. "Tell me, Aurora."

"You've got to promise not to tell him or my mom," Rori said. "They would be devastated. Gwen knows, but she kept the secret all these years."

"So, the attempts Jason and his father made to quiet the story were not successful?" His shrewd guess earned him a nod from Rori.

"It was terrible that first week," she said. "Having Gwen there was the only way I survived. She made me dress up every morning, knowing that my new look would take their shallow minds off my humiliation. There were whispers as I walked into every class. I thought my close friends would rally around me, but they were wary because I had chosen to change my looks so drastically. I thought that they felt like I was trying too hard to be popular...," her words trailed off as the tears started.

Marcus pulled her closer as she relived the high school memory.

"When Jason's dad pulled him off the football team, and he was absent the first few days after Homecoming," she continued, "the rest of the team blamed me and made sure I knew it. The humiliation of being the object of a cruel joke wasn't enough punishment for them. They spread the rumor that my new look was because Jason had..." Her words stopped abruptly.

"Jason had what?" Marcus knew what she was implying, but also knew it was important for her to voice the pain.

"Everyone believed that Jason and I had...," she squeezed her eyes closed, trying to suppress the memories. "That we had...you know...that I was no longer..."

Marcus stopped her. "Rori, look at me." The use of her nickname snapped her out of the haze. "You are not the lie they told. Don't let their evil taint your goodness. You are a beautiful, prized treasure and I will spend the rest of my life convincing you."

Rori let him kiss her softly, then smiled. "You can't go beat them up now," she said. "But thank you for wanting to."

"Did Jason know?" Marcus asked. He was still not sure about the young man's prospects for health and happiness should they ever meet.

"Probably," she said, "but he didn't try to contact me right away. I do think he was truly sorry." She laid her head back on Marcus's chest. "I know I've forgiven him, but Jason was the first guy ever to show an interest in me. When it turned out to be a sham and then when the rumors started," she finished, "I guess the hurt went deeper than I thought." Her honest confession gave Marcus hope.

"Thank you for telling me," he said. "You will have to remind me that I've promised to not injure them if and when we go to your high school reunion, okay?"

"You know," she said, winding her arms around his neck. "It might not hurt for them to be a little scared, though." He laughed and kissed her soundly.

"We better go back in now," Marcus lifted her onto her feet. "Carla about beat me to death when you ran out the door. I think I'll have bruises all over my back. We need to let her know you're okay before she finds a bigger weapon."

He needed to get some space between them too as the resolve he had promised himself, and her father. He was finding it more and more difficult to maintain his distance and self-control. The physical attraction he felt for her was only deepening as he learned about her inner beauty. Now with the clearer story he had, he was terrified of scaring her.

Carla was glad to see they had worked through this crisis, but vowed to keep a close eye on Rori. Having a fun night planned with Jessica would help, she hoped. Tomorrow would be filled with the plans both Mrs. Sinclair and Mrs. MacRae had mapped out. Marcus and

Jake both had duties at the college so they would be out of the way, not that they were sad about missing the shopping trip.

Pastor Sam and his wife met with the young couple on Saturday evening over dinner. They shared some of the pitfalls that they had encountered early in their marriage, counseling Marcus and Rori to spend as much time as they could talking and communicating since they had the added burden of so short a courtship. They needed to spend purposeful time talking to get to know each other before they committed themselves forever.

It was a sobering meeting and both Rori and Marcus were quiet on the way back to Jake's house.

"I know that was kind of scary, Aurora," Marcus turned to her and took both her hands in his after he parked behind Carla's car. "But I promise we will do this right. We both know that God brought us together, no matter how unusual our courtship was. We need to keep trusting that there won't be anything that we face that is not conquerable."

"I still have to remind myself that this is real sometimes," Rori tried to concentrate on her words but was distracted watching Marcus as he toyed with her fingers. She didn't think he realized how just that little motion affected her thinking.

"Oh, it's real, Princess." He leaned his forehead against hers. He would have kissed her, but Jake's porch light flashed on and off suddenly.

"Dad says we have to go in," Marcus grumbled. "I don't want to be on restriction for our wedding week."

Rori giggled but her heart was still troubled. Marcus seemed eager to not be alone with her. She faked sleep on the trip home the next day. She did not want to answer any questions from the two insightful ladies.

The next week was spent packing up her belongings and considering the job opportunities she had been offered. It was a little more difficult since she would be out of the country for three weeks. Thankfully, there was a gallery assistant position in a smaller gallery in town, just around the corner from the Downtown Gallery, and it offered free studio space as a benefit. They were very interested in Rori and were not concerned about the timing of her European trip.

Ten days before the wedding, Rori and her mom were at the bridal shop to pick up the dress. Her gown was a lace-covered vintage halter-top dress that Rori had fallen in love with immediately. She and her mom had visited just three shops and the gown needed very little alteration. It was last year's model and so was less than half what she had thought she would have to spend.

"Almost as if this was meant to be," her mom said mischievously. Rori was still having a hard time accepting that this good fortune was really hers. "You need to relax and let God shower you with this happiness, sweetheart. He is a loving God and you are His daughter. I think He knows that you need all these things to fall into place like this otherwise you would continue to doubt, am I right?" She knew her daughter well.

"Yes," Rori admitted, then got to the real heart of the matter, tears welling in her eyes, "And I miss Marcus."

A quick hug from her mom after the seamstress finished her markings helped tremendously. "You'll see him in a little over a week," her mom reminded her, "and you two talk several times a day, from what I've observed."

"It's not the same," Rori said, "but you're right. It will be okay as soon as I'm back there." Maybe then I can start believing this is all true again, she thought.

Their phone calls usually involved details for the wedding, reception, or honeymoon. What Rori didn't know was that Marcus often invented excuses for their daily calls just to hear her voice. I'm addicted, he told himself. Their text conversations were more playful.

Marcus, did you know that our adventure at Jose's restaurant was our first and only date?

Yes, Aurora, I have realized that. We will have to make up for our unconventional courtship by having lots of post wedding date nights.

You know, there are lots and lots of questions that are normally answered on dates that we haven't covered yet.

Like?

Dogs or cats?

Dogs.

Good.

Really? Would the wedding be called off if I had answered 'Cats'?

Distinct possibility. I'm highly allergic.

Good to know. My turn. Country or Classic Rock?

Yes.

Yes? Both?

What can I say? I have eclectic tastes. You'd also have to add disco, pop, and classical. Leave opera and rap off the list, though.

Oh, well. Guess I'll have to return those Italian opera box seat tickets.

What?!

Joking. Your turn.

Football or baseball?

Soccer. 'Real' football as it should properly be called. And you?

Football. Professional, not college.

Really?

Yes, the whole family are avid fans, Mom especially. Trying hard to picture the demur Mrs. Sinclair rooting loudly for a professional football team, Marcus laughed. He continued the interrogation.

Your turn.

Children?

He was tempted to respond, Yes, but I want you all to myself for at least a year' he thought he'd better not and typed instead, *Yes. How many?*

3, 4, 5...? Rori replied.

Yes! Marcus knew she would sense his obvious enthusiasm. *Names?*

Yes, I think we should name them. Numbers would be silly.

You're tired, dear. Go to sleep. I love you. Ten days.

I love you, too, Marcus. Rori smiled as she added, *nine days…look at the clock.*

She returned to town on Sunday, a week before the wedding. Her car was packed to the roof. Since Marcus had previously hijacked most of her belongings, there was no need for her dad to rent another moving trailer. The rest of her things would fit in the family van that they would bring over on Thursday.

Marcus tried to insist that she stay at the apartment while he bunked with Jake and Carla.

"I would never do that to poor little Zoe," Rori teased him. Despite her continuing doubts, she loved this man so deeply that she had vowed to work on her optimism. She promised herself to choose cheerfulness over questions and humor over seriousness.

"Funny," Marcus retorted.

"I'm staying with Jess until Friday night," she explained. Her parents and sister would be coming into town on Thursday and had rented a suite of rooms at the fancy hotel in town, which was thankfully close to the church. The Saturday evening wedding that had seemed light years away was now almost here.

"We're all set, aren't we?" Marcus interpreted her concerned look as worry over the wedding details.

"Like they say," she smiled at him, "I have the groom and the dress, everything else is gravy."

He laughed and playfully pulled her into a quick hug. "You are delightful and adorable." He kissed her nose. He remembered his news and pulled back to watch her reaction. "All the culinary and art professors have compiled an itinerary for us. Some have even contacted friends along our route and we have reservations at some of the best and some of the little known hidden culinary treasures throughout Europe. You also have a private guided tour scheduled at three very prestigious museums."

He watched as her eyes filled with tears. His dismay was evident. "Why are you crying? That was supposed to be good news!"

"It is." She sniffed. "These are happy tears." He pulled her close and held her while she regained a little composure. He knew that she was emotionally exhausted and was hoping this week did not stress her out any more than was necessary.

After their final meeting with Pastor Sam, mainly to go over the ceremony and vows, Rori saw very little of Marcus that week. Her favorite times were the evenings he spent grading papers and writing out lesson plans for the fall. Being gone for three weeks before you start a new teaching position wasn't ideal, but he was prepared. She sat on the floor in front of his couch working on wedding favors. Just being able to lean against his legs or rest her head on his knee when he took a break was heavenly. She relished this time because she had realized to her dismay that his displays of affection were now becoming more and more infrequent. She struggled anew with doubts about his feelings.

20
Happily Ever After

As the wedding day approached, Marcus tried to insist again that she move into the condominium and let him rent a hotel room.

"Or I can just sleep on the couch at Jake's house," he said.

"Nope," she had teased, "I have no guarantee that you wouldn't sneak in and look at the wedding gown." Nagging doubts still plagued her, too, and she felt like moving into his territory was too bold a move. What if he wanted to change his mind? He would never feel the freedom to do so if she was already entrenched at his house.

Both Carla and Jake grew concerned about Rori as the week went on. They had watched her grow quieter and quieter, especially around Marcus. Her eyes followed him when he wasn't looking, but had a haunted, questioning look. Marcus, on the other hand, could hide his feelings for Rori about as well as a two-year-old trying to keep a secret. His eyes, too, followed his fiancée when she wasn't looking. Only Jake knew how difficult this week had been.

"I'm afraid to even hold her hand," he was painfully honest. "I don't trust myself to not sling her over my shoulder and lock her in the bedroom, marriage certificate or not."

Keeping very little from his wife, Jake shared Marcus's sentiments the night before the rehearsal.

"That's it!" Carla exclaimed. "I know what's wrong with Rori!"

"I'm lost." Jake tried to follow her logic as she explained.

"I think she is interpreting his lack of...how can I put this delicately...physical affection, with disinterest." Jake had just taken a drink of soda and almost choked.

"Disinterest? I won't be explicit, but I'm sure he's definitely *interested.*"

Carla playfully knocked her husband on the head with a pillow. "Behave!" Carla laughed, and then gave her husband strict instructions. "You've got to talk to him before the cookout."

The rehearsal was hectic as most usually were. Carla was astutely aware of Rori's withdrawal. Others most likely were attributing her quietness to exhaustion.

"What's wrong, Rori?" Carla pulled her aside before they headed back to Marcus's for a cookout.

They had picked good old-fashioned American fare since the newlyweds would be immersed in European cuisine for the next three weeks. As a wedding gift, the culinary staff, along with some of their former professors at the culinary institute, had contacted chefs and restaurateurs all along the couple's itinerary. They had reservations, and usually pre-paid meals, at some of Europe's' finest establishments awaiting their arrival.

"Nothing, just tired," Rori said. Tears were forming and she wanted to get away from this very perceptive young wife.

"Liar, liar, pants on fire," Carla mimicked her daughter's singsong voice.

"Is it that obvious?" Rori brushed away tears. As Carla nodded, she continued. "I'm afraid. I think Marcus has changed his mind and now that all these plans are made, he's afraid to tell me."

Carla struggled not to smile. She was pleased with herself that she had 'accurately diagnosed the patient' as Jake would tease her later.

"What makes you think that?" Carla pushed Rori to talk about her concerns. The two walked slightly behind the rest of the crowd making its way up the parking lot.

"He seems to be annoyed whenever I get too close to him," Rori's voice was distressed as she played the last few days over in her mind. "When I got back on Sunday, I practically threw myself at him. He twirled me around once, and then suddenly put me down. It was as if he didn't even like me anymore."

"So, no holding hands, no goodnight kisses?" Carla needed to know the depths of Marcus's depravity. She was going to shake him until his teeth rattled. What was he thinking?

"He does hold my hand, sometimes," Rori admitted, "and kisses me good night, but they're not like, you know." She shrugged slightly.

"Not like a man desperately in love that can't wait for his honeymoon?" Carla finished the sentence for her.

"Exactly," a blushing Rori nodded, head bowed.

"I think you need to talk to him," Carla said as she drove to the condominium. Jake had taken Zoe with him, as they had pre-arranged. He hoped to find a time to set Marcus straight at the cookout.

"I'm afraid he's going to say I'm right," Rori said. "But I guess that's better than forcing him to marry someone he doesn't want anymore."

Rori put on a cheerful front for the group at the rehearsal cookout. Gwen was her maid of honor. Carla and Jess were bridesmaids, and Zoe was the flower girl. Part of her evening was spent sorting out Marcus's brothers James and Collin, along with Saundra, Collin's wife and their five-year-old son, Isaac. Both sets of parents had become good friends, her dad and Marcus's sharing the same dry sense of humor. The laughter from their corner of the patio was interrupted several times with one or the other wife's admonition, "Oh grow up, you two!"

Marcus had given Rori a quick kiss as she came into the kitchen when she and Carla arrived. He had even gently pushed her onto a stool and brushed her hair from her eyes.

"I know you're tired. We can wrap the burgers up and make everyone go home early if you like," he offered.

"You're sweet, but I'm okay," Rori smiled, trying to take encouragement from his tenderness. She leaned toward him, relishing his nearness and attentiveness, but Zoe and Isaac chose that moment to race into the room.

"Aunt Wa-ree!" Zoe tugged on her Rori's ankle length pink sundress, "I-sick says he's the ring bear. What's a Ring Bear?"

Marcus and Rori both laughed, each grabbing a child and swinging them back into the living room. The moment of tenderness was gone.

Rori was so touched from the heart-felt toasts before the meal that she had a hard time keeping the tears from showing. She obediently filled a plate and told Marcus she was going to go out onto the deck, thinking he would join her. Unfortunately, James waylaid him to tend to a minor food mishap. Carla watched the forlorn bride put her plate on a side table and lean on the rail of the deck.

"Do something, now!" Carla whispered frantically to Jake. "Rori is out on the deck, and I'm sure she is crying."

Jake scrambled and grabbed his friend mid-sentence from the kitchen, "Sorry, best man duties," he explained to Rori's mom who was helping Marcus fill more drink glasses. Jake pushed Marcus into the master bedroom and quickly closed the door.

"You, my friend, are a thick-headed clod," Jake folded his arms and dove right into his tirade. "Your wife-to-be is at this moment on the deck, all alone, probably crying, and you want to know why?"

Marcus made for the door, ready to rescue Rori. Jake blocked his way.

"Don't you want to know why?" Jake continued, ignoring the anger he saw rising in his friend's green eyes.

"Why?"

"Because she thinks you don't want her." Jake laid it out as bluntly as he could, knowing time was an issue here.

"Don't want her? What do you mean?"

"Do you need me to draw you a picture?" Jake asked. In a moment, Jake watched the dawning realization on his friend's face.

"Oh, no. I'm an idiot," Marcus said. "And her dad even warned me."

Jake was thankful he hadn't had to go into a lot of detail, since he knew Marcus was trying desperately to maintain self-control around Rori, and now he was being asked to let go of that control. "She thinks you don't find her attractive anymore and that you're just going through with the wedding because you're too afraid of hurting her feelings if you called it off." Jake knew he might be embellishing a little, not knowing Marcus was already convinced.

"Don't find her attractive?" Marcus paled as he was beginning to understand exactly what Dr. Sinclair was communicating. As careful as he had been since then, he had lost sight of how easily Rori's doubts would return. His self-control was meant to show her that his commitment was deeper than attraction. But, as her dad had warned, that restraint had backfired. "So now do I break some rules to convince her?" Marcus shook his head and pushed past his friend.

"I don't think you'll have to break any rules, Marcus. You love her. She just needs to see it, not just hear it," he said. "I'll give you five minutes, and then I'm coming to rescue her," Jake called after him. "Or rescue you," he laughed.

Marcus saw Rori standing alone on the deck. She was resting her chin in her hands as she looked out over the lake that was behind the complex. He realized she had not heard him approach so he quietly stole behind her and put his arms around her, resting his hands on the railing. He effectively had her pinned. She jumped slightly.

"Marcus, you scared me!" She tried to straighten up and turn around, but he seemed to be preventing her from moving.

"Hello, Princess." His voice was low and held a mysterious quality that caused her heart to skip. She could feel his breath on her neck. Her hair was loosely caught up in a clip, just like the first night of class. He desperately wanted to reach up and unclip it but knew his self-control would not be strong enough.

"It has been brought to my attention that you may have misinterpreted my recent actions," he moved his hands ever so slightly closer together. She desperately wanted to lean back into the warmth that she felt radiating from him, but she was still unsure.

"Or should I say, my recent *inactions*," he continued. He heard her breath catch. She tried to turn around. "No, stay put, I won't be able to do this if you're looking at me."

Her shoulders slumped. He realized too late that she misread his meaning. Trying to clear up his statement, he explained.

"I mean you drive me to distraction when you look at me and I need to make myself very clear right now." She seemed to recover, slightly.

"I don't understand," she said softly.

"You know that I've tried as much as I can for the last week to keep my hands to myself, true?" Marcus fought to make sense and not scare her. Deciding to be as honest as possible, he continued. "Despite good advice from your father, and warnings from Jake and Carla, I had no idea you would take my struggle for self-control as me not wanting to marry you." He could see the tears falling silently.

"That could not be further from the truth," Marcus decided it was all or nothing. "I love you, Aurora Grace. I love your kindness, your humor, your giggle, your playfulness, your silliness, and many, many more things. But more than all those together, I love your depth of knowledge of spiritual things, your desire to follow God's will, your love for his people and your love for people who are hurting. I love that you can see the beauty of God in every piece of nature. But," he paused, "those are not the reasons that I love you. There is no logic behind loving you." Rori tensed. "It is beyond logic, beyond words. I can't explain it. It just *is*." He took a deep breath.

"I am amazed and awed that you love me," Marcus said but still did not turn her to face him. He knew if he did, his explanation would be interrupted. "It is only by the grace of our Heavenly Father that I have had the discipline to not break the promises I made to Him to stay pure before marriage." His lips brushed the top of her head. "You have filled my mind for the last six weeks and now that our wedding night is so close, I am clearly on the brink of insanity." Her sobs were audible now.

"Why are you crying?" He turned her around gently and draped her arms around his neck.

"I don't know," Rori clung to him. "I was so scared you didn't want me anymore and were just going to marry me and suffer for the rest of our lives. Everyone has been so kind, but I know they think we're rushing things. But I knew from the first day that this was different. I wanted to love you."

"Despite how awful I was to you?" Marcus wiped her tears. She smiled, knowing his response to her in the beginning was purely defensive.

"I couldn't stop thinking about you and thinking how terrible it would be to have to go on without you." She paused for a breath as her words began to tumble out. "Or worse being married and not ever being able to tell you how you make my knees weak when you look at me and how I just want to run my fingers through your hair and how I think I could kiss you for hours, and..."

"Stop!" Marcus pled for mercy. His resolve was in grave danger. Where was Jake?

Marcus pulled her close and held her face in both hands. He kissed her gently on the forehead, then each tear-dampened eyelid, her nose, and each ear lobe. He finally leaned back. She was clinging to the lapels of his lightweight blazer with both hands, clearly unable to stand on her own.

"I'm going to kiss you now, one last time before we are married, okay?" Marcus draped her hands around his neck and his knees nearly buckled as she lightly ran her fingers along his jaw line and inside the collar of his shirt. "Rori, you're playing with fire now. This is serious."

"Just making sure this was for real," she sighed and leaned her head on his chest. "I thought you said you were going to kiss me."

"Marcus! Time's up!" Jake called from the doorway.

"Go away!" Marcus growled good-naturedly. He called over his shoulder, begging for more time, "I really just finished my explanation and haven't gotten to the demonstration yet."

"You have one minute," Jake retorted mischievously. "Use it wisely, my son!"

Marcus did.

Epilogue

As her father led her into the sanctuary, Rori caught her first glimpse of Marcus. She gasped.

"He's gorgeous!"

The guests had chosen that precise moment to fall quiet, so her spontaneous reaction was heard by most of the guests. Her father laughed as she blushed. Marcus simply grinned and shook his head in amusement.

"You, my friend, are in for a wild ride," Jake laughed. Marcus nodded and smiled even broader.

Rori hesitated, embarrassed at her silly outburst. She saw Marcus raise an eyebrow. He really was unbelievably attractive, she thought. And the kilt was just plain unfair.

"Rori?" Her father's voice woke her from her trance. "I think we need to get going or Marcus may come get you."

"Okay," she whispered. "But he really is gorgeous, you know."

"I know," her father's voice conveyed the humor he saw in the situation. "From the look on his face, I'd say Marcus is thinking the same thing."

An hour later, Marcus found a quiet moment and confirmed her father's observation.

"You, wife, are spectacularly beautiful," Marcus said as he fed her a bite of quiche. "I am flattered that you find my looks tolerable, as you chose so eloquently to point out to all our guests."

"Don't laugh at me!" she said. "I didn't mean to say that out loud. Or at least not loud enough for everyone to hear."

"You are adorable," Marcus said, kissing her gently.

"Thank you for changing out of the kilt," Rori said. "It was quite distracting." Marcus had changed out of the formal Scottish garb into regular trousers. She wasn't about to tell him that she was only slightly less distracted.

"Speaking of distracting, thank you for the warning about your hair." Marcus resisted tugging at the long strands spilling from the clip she now had securely in place.

Rori blushed as she recalled the pre-wedding hair fiasco. Marcus had hinted on several occasions leading up to the wedding that he preferred her hair pinned up. Of course, he failed to tell Rori the reason behind his request. He knew having her long hair unbound for the wedding would be far too tempting for his fragile self-control.

Carla and Jessica tried desperately to get her hair to cooperate. Almost in tears, Rori had told them that Marcus didn't like her hair down and someone needed to warn him that they couldn't get it to work. Carla dissolved into laughter when she realized Rori's misinterpretation and laughed harder as Rori's mom pulled her aside to explain what was really going on. Rori was blushing profusely after the explanation.

"Oh," Rori said quietly. "I guess that could be it. Still, someone needs to warn him." The ladies were able to pull the sides back in long thin braids, but the mass of lovely curls still flowed down her back. There was no other choice given the tiara she was using as a headpiece.

Carla called Jake and tried to explain. She was still laughing but was able to relay the warning. Jake turned to Marcus and donned a solemn look.

"What?" Marcus's imagination ran wild. "She didn't change her mind, did she? She knows I will hunt her down if she does, right?"

"Slow down!" Jake laughed. "No, but I do have some bad news." He loved toying with his friend, so he let his words hang in the air.

"C'mon, Jake," Marcus said. "This isn't funny."

"Carla says they've tried and tried," he paused, "but there's no way to get Rori's hair up for the wedding." Jake laughed as the news sank in and relief washed over Marcus.

"I'm glad you were able to get it pulled up for the reception." Marcus brought her back to the present as he whispered in her ear. "I'm not sure I could have been responsible for my actions otherwise."

After another quick kiss, he stood and bowed, his hand outstretched.

"It's time for the rest of the festivities, my dear," Marcus said. He had seen the gestures coming from his mom and hers. "May I have this dance, Princess?"

"Why yes, Charming." Rori sighed as Marcus took her in his arms for their wedding waltz. He had surprised her by insisting that he choose the song for their first dance. It was a popular love song and she remembered that it had been playing on the radio the rainy night that she had driven him home.

"This song will always remind me of the night I finally admitted that I was falling in lovely with a magical enchantress," he had told her.

"Aurora," Marcus said quietly, halfway through the dance, wanting her full attention.

"Yes, Marcus?" Rori answered wistfully.

"I have a question for you," he said.

"Yes?" She forced herself out of the dreamy state that being in his arms had induced.

"What happened during the ceremony?" His question surprised her, but she knew exactly what he meant.

"What do you mean?" Rori asked, but Marcus could tell by her tone she was feigning ignorance, she wasn't quite ready to explain.

"You know exactly what I mean. I can tell. Since or 'conversation' last night on the deck, I feel like I can almost read your mind, and I know I can read your expressions. So, spill it! What were you thinking during Sam's explanation of the vows? I saw a burden fall away from your shoulders. It was obvious that something he said had a profound impact on you. Tell me, Aurora."

"Oh, Marcus." Tears were threatening, but they were happy ones. "I finally got it."

"Got it?" Marcus asked.

"Sam's talk about the church as a bride and God's love and sacrifice," Rori explained. "True love is a choice, a conscious decision, not an emotion. It doesn't depend on what the other person does."

"This is fascinating, dear," Marcus said. "Please continue."

"Listing what I love about you never made sense," Rori explained. "And definitely thinking what you could possibly love in me was a mystery." She laughed as he frowned at her.

"I heard your words last night, but they didn't sink in completely. During the ceremony, I finally got it." The new bride's eyes were intent on her husband's, trying to make him understand. "I realized that I just love you. As you said, there's no list of reasons, I just do. My love for you is not a feeling. Our love is a choice, but a spiritual one."

"Agreed," he said, "but you still haven't answered my question. What happened during our vows that was such a relief?" Marcus was so intent on his wife's revelation that he didn't realize they had stopped dancing. The wedding guests fell silent as they witnessed what was obviously an important moment.

"I thought I believed it before," the new Mrs. MacRae said, "but at that moment I *knew*."

"Knew what?"

"You love me," Rori stated simply. "You really do love me. Amazing and unbelievable as it seems, I know now with a deep, faith-filled certainty that it's true."

Marcus laughed deeply as he twirled his new bride back into the movement of the dance. As the music ended, he dipped her romantically over his arm.

"Kiss me, Princess Aurora," he commanded.

"Gladly, Chef Charming," Rori said as she eagerly complied.

A Note from the Author

I hope you have enjoyed Marcus and Aurora's story. My good friend Kathy said that their unconventional courtship conveys several important factors in a successful, faith-centered relationship: don't pursue a serious relationship without first knowing the other's faith, set boundaries before the temptation to cross those boundaries is too great, get counsel from friends and family, and *communicate*!

Some may question the speed of Marcus and Rori's relationship, engagement, and marriage. Personally, I think Rori's dad said it best when he told Marcus not to question God's timing. It is after all just that—*God's* timing—not ours.

A family member has painted her interpretation of Rori's painting, *Aurora's Castle*. Check out her Facebook page, Liz Schley Artwork.